VOLUME FIVE

Airship 27 Productions

Domino Lady Volume Five
"The Domino Lady's Daughter" © 2024 Gene Moyers
"The Domino Lady and the Fabergé Egg" © 2024 George Tackes
"The Conqueror's Thorn" © 2024 Gene Popa
"A Girl's Best Friend" © 2024 Fred Adams Jr.

Published by Airship 27 Productions
www.airship27.com
www.airship27hangar.com

Interior and cover illustrations © 2024 Warren Montgomery

Editor: Ron Fortier
Associate Editor: Gordon Dymowski
Marketing and Promotions Manager: Michael Vance
Production Designer: Rob Davis

ISBN: 978-1-953589-66-8

Printed in the United States of America

10 9 8 7 6 5 4 3 2 1

Volume Five
Table of Contents

THE DOMINO LADY'S DAUGHTER

By Gene Moyers

*E*llen Patrick stood up in the tub. Lukewarm bath water cascaded down her slim waist, over seductive hips and down her long, shapely legs. A few bubbles clung here and there as she reached for a large soft towel hanging nearby. Stepping out of the tub onto the soft rug, she patted her torso before lifting one leg to the edge of the tub. She ran the towel along the length of her leg sensuously before switching to the other. Finished, she hung the towel up and reached for the silk dressing gown hanging on the back of the bathroom door.

Ellen crossed the hall to her bedroom belting the silver-colored gown loosely around her. In her bedroom she sat down at her dressing table and picked up her hair brush. Outside the open window the warm breeze brought the sounds of traffic on busy Wilshire Boulevard to her ears. In the mirror her smiling brown eyes stared back as Ellen brushed out her long blonde hair, humming *Isn't it Romantic?* to herself. Finished, she stood up and crossed to her closet. She frowned as he lifted out a dress. Shaking her head, she replaced it and picked out another. Another shake. Another dress. This one was ice blue; long, with a low-cut neckline.

Ellen pulled the silk belt loose and shrugged out of her dressing gown. It slipped to the floor with a whisper. Holding up the dress she crossed to the full-length mirror and held it in front of her. She half closed her eyes imagining how she would look in it. Nodding, she knew it would have the desired effect. She was being taken out to dinner by someone new and she wanted him in the proper frame of mind.

Ellen's date for tonight was a senior aide to a Los Angeles city councilman. He had been around city hall for some time and Ellen hoped he would have lots of inside information on the inner workings of city government. Even better would be some juicy gossip about any of the movers and shakers who came and went in the striking *Hall of Justice* building that dominated LA's skyline. It was information like that gave impetus to her crusade fighting corruption in her beloved Golden State as the mysterious Domino Lady.

She was jerked from her musings by the ringing of the telephone. Throwing the still hangered dress onto the bed she stooped and grabbed up her dressing gown before dashing into the hallway. She had only managed to get one arm in a sleeve and was trying to swing it around her other shoulder as she grabbed up the receiver of the French styled phone on the fourth ring, "Hello!"

There was the briefest of pauses before a brisk, feminine voice asked, "Hello, is this Ellen Patrick?"

"Yes, it is."

The voice then spoke to someone else, "I have your party, now."

There was a 'click' on the line and another female voice spoke rather tentatively, "Hello. Uh, Ellen?"

Ellen answered, "Yes," and waited.

The voice continued, "My name is Tammy Herrold. You may not remember me. It's been a long time but we went to school together some years back at Cal Berkeley."

Ellen frowned. Her mind raced as she shrugged her other arm into the gown, then it clicked and memories fell into place, "Tammy! Of course, I remember you. How long has it been? Five years? You seemed to just disappear one day. Everybody was wondering what had happened to you."

"Well, it's a long story. I uh, did leave Berkeley rather suddenly and I'm sorry I didn't say proper goodbyes. I have fond memories of my time there."

"Yes, they were good. But I hope you've been well. Are you here in LA, now?"

"Well, not quite. I have been well, and I'm really glad I got hold of you."

As Ellen listened, she thought back to her college days in Berkeley. Tammy had been a year or so ahead of Ellen. She had been a quiet, intelligent, studious girl, not give to the fast party life of college. Ellen and others had always thought she seemed kind of sad. At the end of one term, she had simply disappeared without a goodbye to anyone. More interestingly, Tammy and Ellen had not been particularly close. Tammy had not been particularly close to anyone. Why was she calling now?

"It's good to hear from you, Tammy. How did you get my number?"

"Well, I was in town a few days ago and I bumped into Cindy Hansen. We got to talking about old friends and your name came up." Tammy hesitated before continuing, "Cindy happened to mention that you were dating a uh, a private detective."

Ellen frowned; Tammy must be talking about Roger McKane. Roge had lent a hand when Ellen was helping Cindy and her father deal with Charles Mertz and his floating casino. But why would that interest Tammy? "Well, I do know a private detective and he is a good friend. But why would you be interested in private detective?"

There was another pause before Tammy answered in a rather embarrassed voice, "I'm afraid, I've got a problem I need some help with."

Ellen raised an eyebrow as she replied, "It must be a serious problem if you need a detective. Can you tell me about it?"

"Umm, it's not the kind of thing I want to talk about on the phone and I don't have too much time. I have to go soon but I do need your help. Can you give me the number of your detective friend?"

"I can. But I would like to hear why you need help. I'll gladly talk to Roge for you but it would help if I know a little more."

Another pause followed before Tammy agreed, "Alright. Can you come and meet me, on Monday?"

"Certainly, but why not tomorrow or Sunday?"

"I'm afraid I am very busy on the weekends. Monday is the soonest I can see you."

"Okay. Where do we meet?'

"I'm afraid I live in Santa Barbara. I know it's a long trip for you but I don't know when I'll be back in the city."

Somewhat surprised Ellen agreed, "Sure I can drive up to Santa Barbara Monday. Where do I go?"

Tammy quickly gave Ellen an address and then thanked her sincerely before hanging up. Ellen thoughtfully hung up her phone. As her alter ego, Domino Lady she lived the exciting life of an adventuress. Pursuing corrupt officials or helping out old friends for the sake of adventure. She used a portion of any funds she recovered from the corrupt to fund her fast life style. The remainder she funneled toward worthy charities. Now, it seemed she would be helping another old friend; a rather mysterious one it seemed.

Monday morning found Ellen driving up the coast highway. Santa Barbara was nice little town of just over thirty-thousand people north of Los Angeles nestled along the beautiful California coast. Just under a hundred miles north of downtown Los Angeles along Hwy 101 it was a bit of a drive but Ellen had left early and took her time. The top on her roadster was down to allow the beautiful spring day to beam down on her. To keep her lush head of blonde hair under control hair she had a scarf tied across it. The journey was pleasant. She took her time, enjoying the spectacular coastal scenery.

After a stop for a leisurely lunch in Ventura, Ellen motored on and arrived in Santa Barbara before three o'clock. It took only minutes to find the location that Tammy had given her. As she pulled her roadster up behind a line of parked cars along East Sola Street, she noted the time; 3:10 pm. She opened her door and stepped out. Frowning, she noted people waiting in the cars along the sidewalk. Ellen walked forward along the sidewalk. As she did, somewhere a bell began to ring. Moments later, laughing children began to stream out of wide double doors onto the sidewalk. Ellen stopped as children streamed past her. Above the doors, carved into the stone she read; *The Dolores School*. Underneath was carved, *Our Lady of Sorrows Parrish*. Turning her head Ellen noted the large white-washed Catholic Church with its tall single bell tower next door. That was no doubt *Our Lady of Sorrows*.

Ellen frowned as she looked around. Tammy had told Ellen to meet her here at 3:15. Perhaps she was picking up her child. She scanned the autos into which children were climbing, but saw no one who was interested in her. Turning back, she saw a nun was holding the door open and speaking briefly to some children as they left the building. They waved and called out as they reached the sidewalk and broke apart in all directions. She looked at the nun who looked directly at her before waving a friendly arm in her direction.

Surprised, Ellen walked toward the school. She could not make out any details about the nun dressed in her full length, black habit but she did note the young face smiling at her. As she neared the steps the young nun spoke, "Hello, Ellen. It's good to see you again."

Ellen's steps faltered. Her mouth dropped open. Her foot reaching for the next step stopped in mid-air. She could not keep the surprised look from her face, "Tammy?"

The young nun smiled, "Yes, Ellen. It's been such a long time."

Ellen took two more steps to stand next to her old friend. As she did, she thought back. She shook her head, "Nearly six years. And I see things have changed."

Sister Tammy brushed at the front of her robes, "Yes, some things may have changed. But not you. You're as lovely as ever and leading such a gay and exciting life or so Cindy Hansen claims."

Seeing the familiar smile and hearing her old friend spoke made Ellen want to reach out and hug her. She smiled somewhat doubtfully and said as much.

Tammy laughed and held her arms out saying, "Hugs are allowed between old friends. The church allows dispensations."

Ellen hugged her friend hard, whispering, "It's wonderful to see you!"

Releasing the young nun, Ellen said, "I have so many questions I want to ask."

Sister Tammy nodded, "Yes, I'm sure. But the steps of the Parrish school are not the place for them. Follow me; I know a quiet place where we can talk." Turning she led the way through the double doors into the school. A short hall led to a wider crossing hall that ran both ways. She led the way left passing now empty class rooms. The few students they passed smiled and sang out, "See you tomorrow, Sister" or "Goodbye Sister, Tammy," as they passed. Tammy answered them happily. It was plain to Ellen that Sister Tammy was popular with the students here. As they reached a heavy door at the end of the hallway, Ellen remarked, "The children all seem to like you a lot."

Sister Tammy pushed open the door and let Ellen through before closing it behind them, "The children are so wonderful. I love teaching them. I sometimes feel like they are all my own children."

The young sister sounded so sincere that Ellen looked at her, as they walked along a covered breezeway toward the church. "I went to public school but I always heard stories of how hard the nuns were at parochial schools."

Sister Tammy laughed, "They probably studied under Sister Agnes or someone similar. Some of the older sisters here take discipline very seriously. I believe discipline should always be tempered with understanding and love."

Ellen marveled at this mature sentiment as Tammy stepped up several stone steps and pulled open heavy door near the front side of the church. The two found themselves in a dimly lighted vestibule. To their left stone steps spiraled out of sight upwards. Tammy led the way past this into a corridor that led to the narthex. To their left the multiple, outer church doors were closed. To the left the wide doors leading to the nave were open wide. Sister Tammy led the way through narthex. Before entering the nave she stopped at the font, dipped her fingers and crossed herself while curtsying.

The church was impressive. The ceiling was high and vaulted. Illumination was dim, although colored light from the large stained-glass window high above the main doors filtered past them from behind. The Chancel was brighter. Ellen could see someone sitting in one of the front pews praying. Tammy led them to a row on the right about halfway up the right side. They slid into the pew and sat down. Tammy bowed her head for a few seconds, then looked at Ellen, "I suppose, you first want to know, how I went from Berkeley to a nunnery and then here."

Ellen nodded, "It was a bit of a shock, at first. You weren't one of the "good time girls" at school. But it is still surprising to find you here. It's a long way from Berkeley."

Tammy hesitated for a moment before speaking, "I wanted to go to college to be a teacher since I was a little girl. When my father died, it looked like my dreams might not work out. Then…something happened. I got to go to school but it was always bitter sweet. It never held as much joy as I thought it would."

"Is that why you disappeared so quickly after you graduated. Several of the girls wondered what had happened to you."

"Yes. That's part of it. I also had to think…to decide my future."

Ellen waited patiently. It was obvious that Tammy had something important to get off her chest. She could not be hurried. After a few moments, the young nun continued, "School was great, I loved learning and studying but it was not as much fun as it should have been." She turned and looked at Ellen in the dim light. "I know that sounds childish. I was there to learn but I had a lot on my mind that often kept me from enjoying the experience as much as you and some of our friends did." She sighed softly. "I envied you the care free lives you had, your ability to enjoy the wonderful experience of college life."

Remembering how sad Tammy had often seemed at school, Ellen asked, "What was bothering you so much back then, Tammy?"

"I had a lot on my mind, then." There was the slightest of pauses. "I'm afraid I was always thinking of my daughter." Ellen nearly dropped her purse at this shocking revelation. Her mind raced as she tried to think of what to say. Tammy looked at her and even in the dim light Ellen could see how sad she looked. "I know you must be shocked; but it's true. I had a young daughter even then."

"How could that be? You were so young." Even as she spoke Ellen heard the naiveté in her words. It was too obvious what must have happened. She quickly added, "How stupid of me, Tammy. I'm sorry. Can you. . . tell me about it?"

"It happened when I was in high school. After Dad died, things were hard for Mom and me. Dad left a small amount of insurance but Mom had to take a job. She also took in ironing to make extra money on the side. I helped with that and I baby sat after school for neighbors. We managed to keep things together but I knew there wasn't going to be any money for college. Still, I worked hard to keep my grades up."

Ellen thought to herself about the cost of an education at an expensive school like Berkeley but saved her questions to let Tammy tell her story. "Then it happened. Things went out of control and suddenly, I'm pregnant." She was silent for a moment, "I dropped out of school until after she was born. Then went back and graduated."

Ellen asked cautiously, "What happened to the baby?"

"There was private adoption, arranged by a lawyer. I only saw her once and then she was gone." Another sigh came from Ellen's old friend. Multiple questions bubbled to Ellen's lips. First; "And the father?"

"I never saw him again. I was to never try and see him or say anything. It was part of the agreement the lawyer arranged. He paid for the lawyer and gave us enough money for my mother to send me to Berkeley. All in exchange for keeping things quiet."

Ellen cocked her head to one side, "You mean his parents paid, don't you? They must have insisted on the adoption. But what about him? Didn't he love you?"

Tammy's head bowed. "He said he did but I know now he was lying." She hesitated then whispered, "He was married. The baby had to be adopted. His wife insisted."

Ellen was thunder struck. For a moment she didn't know what to say. When she got her voice back, she asked, "Who was he? How did you meet him?"

"I was their baby sitter." The simple words hit Ellen with the crash of metal beams dropped on concrete. Her mind reeled for a moment. When she finally spoke, she tried to hold her temper in check. "So, this man, the father of your child was an older, married man that you babysat for?"

"Yes. They lived down the street. They were pretty well off. He was a lawyer and she came from money, I guess."

Ellen frowned as she asked quietly, "When was this?"

"Before my senior year of high school."

"So, you were what? Sixteen? Seventeen?"

Tammy nodded looking forward, "Yes, just before my seventeenth birthday?" Ellen was silent. She could feel her temper rising. She clenched her hands in her lap. She knew if she could see herself, she would be red with anger. Tammy mistook Ellen's silence for judgement, "I know; I was stupid. I think of how he told me all those lies and what a fool I was to believe he loved me...you must think I was such a little idiot...or worse."

"No, Tammy! I do not think any of that! You are not to blame here. It's him, this...this sad excuse for a man. He was older, and married. He should have known better. He took advantage of a young girl, lied to her and when he got her in trouble, he bought his way out. He's...contemptible! You do realize you were under age back then. What he did was illegal as well as just plain wrong!"

"But, I should have known...been stronger."

"Tammy, you are not to blame for this! It is not your fault. It's his!" Ellen paused, "Is this why you wanted to see me? To tell me about this horrible man?"

Tammy shook her head, "No. I have long since forgiven him for his wrongs as the Lord has forgiven me. What I wanted to talk to you about was this friend you're dating. Cindy Hansen said he was a private detective."

Ellen pursed her lips. Cindy had met Roge McKane when Ellen had been helping her out with a small blackmail problem the year before. It probably was natural for her to think that Ellen and he were a couple. "Well, actually Roge and I don't have any commitments. We are close though. He's a lot of fun to be with and he is as dependable as the sun coming up. But why would you want me to introduce you to him?"

"Ellen, I am very happy here. I love the church and all my students. I wouldn't change any of that. But I often think of my little daughter. Late at night I lie awake and wonder what happened to her. I wonder what her name is and what she looks like. Most of all, I wonder if she's happy." She leaned toward Ellen and picked up her hand, "I don't want to interfere in whatever life she has now, but I would like to know what happened to my little girl. If your friend can help me find her, I would be eternally grateful." She hesitated before adding, "I'm afraid I don't have very much money but I do have a little I've saved and…"

Ellen squeezed her friend's hand, "Don't worry about money, we'll figure all that out later. You just tell me what you need to know and I'll get people looking, okay?"

"Oh, Ellen! Thank you, you don't know how much I've prayed for the Lord to help me. When I heard about you and your friend from Cindy, I knew the Lord had answered my prayers!"

Ellen hid her smile, thinking, *If the Lord sent the Domino Lady to help Tammy then the caped adventurer must be on the side of the angels.* To Tammy she said, "I don't know if the angels sent me but I'll do what I can. Now tell me everything you can remember about the adoption and this worm of a man."

Tammy sat up straighter and her voice was more certain as she spoke, "Alright, I don't know much but I have the papers my Mom left me when she died last year."

"Good. That's a place to start. Now, I have some questions that my friend Rog will want to know…"

It had been a long drive home. The good thing was Ellen had had time to digest all that Tammy had told her. She was still steamed at the sordid story she had been told when she walked through the door of her fourth floor, Wilshire Boulevard apartment. She needed to relax and think.

Ellen walked into her bedroom and quickly shed her clothes. Naked she stretched her arms over her head and stood on tip toes working the kinks out. She then walked naked down the hall to the bathroom. There, she turned faucets and soon had steaming water running into the tub. She added some bubble bath solution and bath salts, then left for the kitchen. It was the work of only two minutes to open a bottle of champagne. Grabbing a glass, she was soon on her way back to the bathroom.

Turning off the water, Ellen lifted a shapely leg over the side of the tub and stepped in. She eased herself down into the hot water and leaned back. Closing her eyes, she thought back to all that had happened that eventful day. Opening her eyes, she reached for the bottle next to the tub and poured herself a glass of bubbling liquid. As she sipped the dry, cold champagne she planned.

She had perused the papers Tammy had given her during a quick stop on the drive home. The adoption papers signed by both Tammy and her mother, as legal guardian, gave no names and few details but the lawyer himself was the place to start. Roge could probably help out there. Also listed was the legal father. That was important. Ellen had already decided that the Domino Lady was going to track down the snake of a philandering husband that had victimized poor Tammy. When she did, the mysterious avenger would definitely have words for that loathsome cad. Ellen sipped her champagne as she luxuriated in the steamy water. If this lothario thought he was a lady's man then the Domino Lady should definitely make his acquaintance.

"Roger McKane, here."

"Hold for a long-distance call, please."

Surprised, Roge waited for a moment as the long-distance operator connected him with his caller. Seconds later a familiar, sexy voice said, "Ooohhh, I love it when you're so official."

"Ellen! Tell me you're here in San Fran. I badly need an excuse to escape all this paper work."

A laugh came over the line, "I'm not there now, but there is a possibility I can come for a visit soon, especially if you can help me out with a small favor."

Roge didn't need to pretend to be suspicious; favors for Ellen had a way of getting complicated quickly. He asked innocently, "And just what kind of trouble are you getting me into this time?"

"Oh, Roge! I'm hurt that you think I would be up to no good. Have I ever asked for anything that was unreasonable?"

"Uh, huh. But tell me what it is anyway. You know I can't refuse you anything."

Ellen laughed, an honest, music like sound, "Thanks Roge. I need to find out about a lawyer named Isaac Cohen. He's practicing somewhere in the Bay area. I need his address and any information you can find about him."

"Why, do I think this is going lead to trouble?"

"Trouble? No trouble, Roge. Just trying to locate this lawyer for an old friend. And, if you find out anything interesting, it might be worth a trip up to hear what you have to say…personally," Ellen teased playfully.

Roge laughed, "Well, I better get right on that." After a few more pleasantries, the two said their goodbyes and hung up. It hadn't been too hard to find out about Isaac Cohen the lawyer who had handled the long-ago adoption of

Ellen sipped her champagne.

Tammy's young child. Rather than make official inquiries through the State Bar Association, Ellen made a few local calls. Sure enough, one of her lawyer contacts remembered an Isaac Cohen practicing somewhere in the Bay Area. This was quite convenient; for Ellen's long-time friend Roger McKane was an up and coming operative for a well-known San Francisco detective agency. She had no doubt he would be able to track down Isaac Cohen in short order.

While Roge was busy detecting, Ellen decided to begin the second half of her carefully thought-out plan.

The next day found Ellen sitting in her roadster on *Crenshaw* a busy street in the heart of *Inglewood*, just south of Los Angeles proper. *Inglewood* was about twelve miles south of downtown LA and perhaps nine miles directly south of Ellen's Wilshire Blvd apartment. She was watching the storefront campaign headquarters of Nathan Whitaker who was running for his second term in the State Assembly. There was a local train that ran from downtown out to Inglewood and beyond to the coast but she had decided to drive her roadster for its versatility. Arriving late in the morning she had watched the campaign HQ for an hour then had lunch in a nearby diner. As she had hoped several campaign workers lunched there and she listened carefully for gossip and other useful information.

After another day of watching, Ellen decided it was time to approach the headquarters for a closer look and perhaps a meeting with the assemblyman. Ellen left her car and being careful of traffic, crossed the street and walked toward the headquarters. She wore a conservatively cut dress and sensible low heels. Her purse was of good quality but slightly worn. She wanted to look attractive but no nonsense. It wouldn't do to appear too anxious. She did not want to make the wrong impression.

Reaching the glass door of the storefront, she paused to touch her hair and make sure it was smooth then took a breath and pushed through into the interior. Inside the floor was wide open. Desks and tables were scattered everywhere. Large posters proclaiming "Re-Elect Whitaker for State Assembly" lined the walls. Many of these had the oversized black and white image of a smiling man beaming out at the room. Boxes of supplies were piled everywhere and some of the half dozen people milling about were busy loading or unloading posters, flyers and various office supplies from these boxes. Others answered phones or were typing busily. At the back of the large room, a temporary partition had been erected. Several doors were open and Ellen could see desks and tables within some of them.

As she stood there looking around, a man in shirt sleeves rolled up to his elbows saw her. He stood up from a desk and came forward. He was a middle aged, slightly balding man with average looks but sharp eyes that quickly sized up Ellen. He smiled carefully and asked, "May I help you, miss?"

Ellen pasted a slightly embarrassed look on her face and spoke, "Uh, hello. My name is um, Ellen Hale."

She paused for a moment and the man in front of her tried to put her at ease by holding out his hand, "Miss Hale, I'm Fred Harris, Assemblyman Whitaker's campaign chairman. What can we do for you today?"

Ellen shook the hand hesitantly. "Well, I live here in the district and I would like to volunteer for the re-election campaign.

Harris' smile grew wider as he nodded, "That's great! We can use all the help we can get. Where do you live?"

Ellen had done her homework and named an address in a nearby residential neighborhood. Harris nodded and sized her up, "Good. What kind of skills do you have?"

"Well, I can type, take short hand and I'm not afraid of hard work. I'll do whatever is needed. Stuffing envelopes or handing out flyers is fine with me."

Before Harris could answer a confident voice spoke up from behind him, "That's just the kind of enthusiasm we need around here." Harris and Ellen turned. A tall, lean man, his dark hair slicked back from his high forehead had come up silently behind Harris and was smiling at the two of them.

Harris, said, "This is Miss Hale, Nathan. She's here to volunteer."

"So, I heard. It sounds like she's just what we need around here. Hard working, enthusiastic believers are what is going to win this campaign for us."

Whitaker stepped forward and offered his hand. Ellen took it and met his smiling gaze. The Assemblyman was thirty-six years old, handsome with dark, wavy hair with an open winning smile. Ellen dropped her eyes and blushed slightly as she shook his hand. Although, he kept his eyes on her face, it was obvious that he had missed nothing about Ellen's appearance or good looks. She smiled shyly. "It's a real pleasure to meet you Mr. Whitaker. You've done such a wonderful job representing us, here in Inglewood."

"Why, thank you so much. And please call me Nathan." Letting go of her hand that he had held just a moment too long, he turned to his manager, "I'm sure we can find some work for Miss, uh...?"

Ellen spoke up, "Hale. Ellen Hale."

"Fine. It was a pleasure meeting you, Ellen. I'll leave you in Fred's capable hands. I'm sure we'll see more of you soon." Whitaker moved off toward the rear partitioned offices exchanging word with other volunteers as he passed.

Harris smiled at Ellen. "Well, it looks like you're on the team. When can you start?"

Ellen frowned, "I'd like to start tomorrow, but I'm driving my mother back home this weekend. Is Monday soon enough?"

"Monday will be fine. We'll see you bright and early then."

"Alright. I'm really looking forward to working with the assemblyman. I'm sure it will be a wonderful experience working here."

Harris nodded. "I'm sure Nathan will be glad to have you here and be very grateful for your efforts."

Ellen thanked him again and took her leave. Outside, as she walked back to her car she thought. Whitaker was definitely a lady's man. With his good looks and smooth manner, it was no surprise that he could easily take advantage of an innocent young girl. He had not even tried to hide his admiring estimation of her. Opening the driver's door, she tossed her purse onto the seat and lifted a long leg into the car. Slamming the door, she thought herself, *If he's already interested, it will make things easier.*

The car started Ellen engaged the gears and pulled away from the curb feeling alive and excited. The excitement of the chase flowed through her and she smiled as the wind whipped her hair in the wind stream of the roadster.

Bright and early the next morning, Ellen left for the long drive north to San Francisco. After her little visit to meet the Assemblyman, she had returned home in time to receive a long-distance call from Roge. He had located Attorney Cohen and was anxious to parlay his new knowledge into a visit from Ellen. Ellen for her part was happy to oblige. It had been some months since she had visited the city by the Bay and time with Roge was always pleasant. Arrangements were made and she turned to packing. She had just the new dress she was dying for Roge to see her in.

It was nearly a ten-hour drive, counting a lunch stop along Hwy 99 in the Central Valley, and the ferry ride across the bay, and Ellen was very tired when she finally pulled into the forecourt of the *Mark Hopkins Hotel.* A uniformed valet took her car while a bell hop carried her luggage in to the lobby. Ellen had stayed at *The Mark* before. Built on the site of the original Mark Hopkins mansion, and completed just six years before, the luxury hotel was already becoming a San Francisco landmark. Management had her phoned in reservation and she was quickly shown to her suite. After the long road trip Ellen drew a hot bath for herself. She badly wanted a drink from room service but *The Mark* was far too elegant to be caught violating prohibition. Instead, she soaked the miles away while her stomach growled from inattention.

Later, wrapping a robe around her svelte figure, Ellen made a phone call. It was after business hours so the number she dialed was Roge's home number. He answered on the second ring, "Ellen! Tell me you're here in town."

She laughed, "Of course, I am darling, Roge."

"Are you at *The Mark Hopkins?*"

"Now, where else would I be, silly. I'm here and starving."

"Of course. I suppose there is time for a late dinner." He looked at his watch. It was after eight o'clock. "In fact, I know a little place you'd love. And we probably won't need a reservation."

"Good. Come and get me before I collapse from hunger."

"I'll be there in a jiffy."

Hearing the excitement in his voice, Ellen laughed as she hung up the phone. Suddenly excited herself, she exclaimed, "I'd better hurry!" and hurried toward the bedroom.

Setting her fork down, Ellen sighed and leaned back in the booth, "That was wonderful." She lifted her glass. Roge leaned forward and clinked his against it. They were in a secluded booth in the back of a quaint restaurant near the bay. Roge knew the management and a discreet exchange of money had secured them a good, but illegal bottle of wine. Dinner had been pleasant with the two of them exchanging gossip and catching up on their lives. Now conversation turned to Ellen's current business.

"So, what have you got yourself into, this time, Ellen?"

"It's nothing. I'm just trying to locate a lawyer for an old friend."

"It's a long way to go for a lawyer. What's so special about this Cohen guy?"

"Well, he did some work for my friend's mother years ago before she died. My friend is just trying to find out some details from him."

Roge looked suspicious, "It's not anything like that gambling deal last year is it?"

"No. Definitely not. This is just me helping get a hold of this lawyer for a friend who can't do it herself."

"Okay, I've located him. He's actually just quite close by."

"Really! Where?"

"He has an office over in Oakland. Been there for years."

"Really? That's great! Any good dirt on him?"

"Not really. He specializes in family law. You know, wills, trust, estates, that sort of thing. Everybody I talked to says he's a straight arrow type."

"That's good to hear. I knew you would come through, Roge."

The detective smiled modestly, "Thanks." He then gave her a knowing look, "I know you're going to want to rush over and talk to him but tomorrow but I was hoping we'd have some time for ourselves."

Ellen looked directly at him, "There's no need for me to talk to Mr. Cohen, personally. I'll pass his address along to my friend and that'll be it."

"Good. I can get tomorrow off and we'll do the town. Does that sound good?"

Ellen reached across the table and placed her hand over Roge's, "Absolutely."

Two nights later, the last thing on Ellen's mind was the pleasant day she had spent with her friend. Instead, she was looking for traffic along a side street in downtown Oakland. The street was quiet. Opening her car door, she slipped out onto the dimly lit street and quietly closed it behind her. Pulling her long black cloak around her she walked casually across the street. On the other side she looked around carefully before slipping into a darkened alley.

While her eyes adjusted to the gloom of the alley, she slipped a black domino mask from under her cloak over her face. Turning the Domino Lady stepped across the alley to the back of the *Farley Building*. Above her the metal fire escape hugged the rear of the building just inside the alley's mouth. Just out of reach, stretched a long ladder held horizontal by heavy counter weights. Pulling out a small metal grappling hook attached to a heavy cord from beneath her voluminous cloak the Domino Lady swung it back and forth a few times before swinging it upward to loop over one of the lower rungs of the metal ladder.

The noise it made was surprisingly loud in the empty alley but the masked woman ignored that as she pulled down strongly on the cord. The ladder tipped and swung down toward the ground with the slightest of metallic squeaks. She grabbed it before it hit the ground easing it to the alley floor. Coiling up the cord, she quickly climbed up the ladder to the second-floor landing.

Ellen Patrick had made a foray to the Farley building earlier that day. Normally, she would enter a building like this before it closed and hide in one of the bathrooms or broom closets until after closing. Unfortunately, the Farley building was locked on Saturdays. Anyone working on Saturday was admitted by a security guard. She hadn't had time to arrange an appointment so her normal admittance was denied her. Fortunately, the Domino Lady was very familiar with fire escapes and this one proved to be little hindrance to her.

Lifting her long white dress hem with one hand she climbed quickly to the fourth-floor landing. There she bent down on one knee and peered through the window. It opened onto a lighted hallway. The window was locked but a quick manipulation of the twist latch with a lock pick and the Domino Lady was able to lift the sash and soundlessly slip inside. Closing the window behind her, she turned and walked up the short hall to where it met a long hall running the width of the building.

Flipping a mental coin, she turned left and moved off down the hall noting office numbers as she went. Quickly she realized the numbers were running in the wrong direction from the office number listed in the Oakland phone book. Turning around she quickly retraced her steps past the rear hallway where she had entered. Two offices later the corridor turned sharply to the left, paralleling the side street outside. A few doors down she reached the office she was looking for.

The door was on her right. The upper half of the hall door was of frosted glass. Painted in black on the glass were the words; *Isaac Cohen* and below that, *Attorney at Law*. The Domino Lady again produced her trusty lock pick. Dropping to one knee she went to work on the door. Moments later, the lock clicked back and she stood up stretching her back. As she turned the door knob, the metallic clang of a door closing from somewhere on the floor came to her ears.

Pushing into the darkened office, Domino Lady softly closed the door behind her and turned the twist lock. She stood silently her ear near the door listening for several minutes. Only silence came to her ears. Probably only a janitor or late worker entering a stairwell, she finally decided. Using a small pencil flashlight, the masked avenger sized up her surroundings. She was in an outer office fitted out as a waiting room with a sofa, armchairs and a secretary's desk. A typewriter stood on a small portable table next to the desk.

Nothing interesting would be found here. Her light quickly found the inner door marked *Private*. This door too was locked. The Domino Lady's pick made short work of it. Inside the inner office and away from the hallway, she felt confident enough to flick on the overhead lights. A large desk with a comfortable leather chair dominated room, with a window behind it. Two comfortable armchairs sat in front of the desk. A glass fronted bookshelf filled with expensive, leather-bound law books was against the right-hand wall. A leather sofa ran along the left side wall. Most importantly, a waist high, steel safe sat in the far rear corner of the room. Three tall, filing cabinets took up the other rear corner.

The safe would be very tempting to any normal cat burglar but the Domino Lady was here for information not loot. She glided quickly to the file cabinets. The middle cabinet was the one she wanted. It took only a minute to find the file she was looking for. Knowing that adoption records were considered confidential, she had known that the only way she was going to get the information she needed was to break in this way. Regrettable, but she was removing nothing and her late-night visit would go unknown with a bit of luck.

The file she wanted was listed under Tammy's mother's name. It contained various documents and signed papers, including a copy of the baby's birth certificate listing the father's name. The masked woman lifted an eyebrow at this and smiled thinly. Official documentation like that might come in handy later. Most importantly the file contained the name and address of the couple that had adopted Tammy's daughter. This crucial information was hurriedly scribbled down on a notepad from the desk. The file was quickly returned to its place and the Domino Lady moved toward the outer door. At the last second, she turned back and tore several pages from the notepad she had used. This removed any impressions her writing had made to the sheets of the notepad.

Reaching the door, she turned off the lights and re-entered the outer office. It was the work of only a minute to re-lock the inner office door before she glided silently across the darkened office to the outer hallway door. Filtered light passing through the frosted upper half dimly lit area around the door. Domino Lady put her ear to the crack between the door and jamb and closing her eyes listened carefully. A full minute passed and she heard nothing alarming. Opening the door, she peered out carefully. The hallway in both directions was empty.

Slipping out Domino Lady closed the door quietly and dropped to one knee to re-lock the door. As she inserted her pick in the lock she startled by a shout, "Hey!" Startled, she dropped the pick to the floor. A glance to her left showed a man standing at the end of the corridor where it bent around to the front of the building. He was wearing a blue uniform and a matching cap. In one hand was flashlight. From his Sam Browne belt hung a flap holster. All this Domino Lady took in instantly. As she grabbed up her lock pick the man shouted, "What are you doing?"

Considering her mask and current position this seemed a silly question to the Domino Lady but she did not stop to think about it. Knowing she couldn't beat the security guard to the rear fire escape and being even more certain she did not want a violent confrontation, the Domino Lady did the only practical thing. As the security guard broke into a run, fumbling with his holster, she opened the door to Cohen's office, stepped in and closed it behind her.

Flipping the lock up, she turned and swiftly crossed to the inner office. By the time the guard had reached the outer door and was rattling the door knob she was busy working on the inner lock again. Ignoring the guard's shouts and pounding on the door, she worked swiftly. Her heart was beating loudly and she found herself holding her breath but the masked intruder worked confidently and seconds later the lock yielded. As she entered the inner office and locked the door behind her, the guard yelled through the outer door, "Don't move! You're trapped!" Chillingly, she could hear keys rattling as he searched for the correct pass key.

The masked avenger did not hesitate. There was no other choice. She quickly crossed the room and around the desk to the window. Turning the latch, she lifted the sash and thrust her head and shoulders through the window. The cool night air hit her face. Before her yawned open space. She did not glance down. She knew there was nothing but sidewalk forty feet below broken only by a narrow ledge that ran along the building just below the window sill. The foot-wide ledge was not as wide as he had hoped but wider than she had feared. Letting out her held breath, she looked to her right. The ledge ran for thirty feet and then followed the corner of the building into the alley. Behind her the inner door rattled. Through it came shout, "I'm calling the police!" Ignoring the distraction, she slowed her breathing and cleared her mind.

Taking a deep breath Domino Lady lifted one foot and slipped off her high heel. She quickly repeated this with the other foot. She then pushed her upper head and shoulders through the window. Carefully she edged her upper body through the window and to the right along the ledge. Setting down a heel on the ledge, she reached back and hiked her long dress up around her waist. Her long legs free, she grabbed up the heel and carefully got a knee over the sill and onto the ledge. She followed this with the other knee. Spreading her arms wide she turned carefully to get her back around toward the wall.

The next step was the hardest. Ignoring more shouts through the locked inner door, she carefully pushed herself upright. Now on her knees with her lower legs inside the office and her back against the window, she slowly lifted one foot and got it to the sill. Pressing back against the window she slowly pushed herself up. Seconds later she was upright. Her arms spread wide and pressed against the window and wall. In each hand she held a heeled pump.

Keeping her head up so as not to look down at the ground, the Domino Lady carefully slid her right foot along the stone ledge. Her left foot followed. Grateful that there was only a light wind on this spring night, she slowly moved away from the window. Moving steadily but carefully she sidestepped along the ledge.

Seconds later her right hand felt open air. She had come to another window. Here the inset of the glass window gave her a precious few more inches of room. She stopped there for a few seconds to rest before she continued her perilous journey. Turning her head, she saw that the corner was closer but still seemed miles away. She reminded herself to breathe and continued.

In the distance she could hear traffic noises. Horns honking, engines

In each hand she held a heeled pump.

revving but no sirens…yet. Suddenly a gust of wind swirled down the street. She was pressed firmly back against the building but the wind caught her long dress and lifted it, swirling it above and around her waist. Her cloak pressed between her and the wall flapped around her. The masked woman froze. The long dress acted as a flag tugging at her, pulling her away from the wall toward oblivion. Bracing her feet, she pressed her back as hard as she could against the wall. Her dress flapped and waved but moments later the gust was past and her dress settled against her legs.

Softly cursing the ever-changing bay area weather, Domino Lady let out her held breath and muttered, "I'm a lady thief, not some second story man. This is undignified." She continued her along her dangerous path. Seconds later her right hand moved into open air; she had reached the corner.

This would be the hardest part. She had to edge around the sharp corner without losing her balance. Edging one foot around the corner she moved slowly, praying another gust of wind didn't happen along when her back was to the sharp corner and she was most away from the steadying wall. As she pivoted carefully around the corner there came to her ears the sound of a distant siren. Ignoring it, she pushed herself gently around the corner until she was once more against flat wall.

It was mercifully dark in the alley and she instantly felt better knowing that she wasn't visible to anyone glancing up from the street. The siren was getting louder. She didn't have the luxury of waiting for her eyes to adjust to the darker alley. She continued side stepping along the ledge toward the dimly lit fire escape. She winced as her bare foot stepped down on a pebble or other minor obstruction but continued her teeth pressed hard together. Light escaping the rear corridor reflected off the metal framework.

When she was ten feet away from the fire escape, the masked woman gently tossed the high heel in her right hand onto the metal landing. It landed with a muted clang. Edging closer she tossed the other. Finally, she was three feet away. Turning slightly, she pushed off into space with a leap. Her hands caught the railing and one foot the metal landing. The other the foot slipped off into space but she held on to the rail easily and quickly pulled herself over into the landing with a sigh of relief.

The siren went silent. The cops were out front and would soon be pounding up the steps. Her shaking hands found her heels and slipped them on, ignoring the runs in her silk stockings. A glance through the window showed an empty rear corridor. She turned and slipped down the ladder toward the next landing.

A minute later she was on the pivoting ladder swinging down to the alley floor. She jumped off and ignored the loud "clang" the ladder made as it swung back into position, as she hurried to the alley mouth. The side street was empty. In the distance she could hear another siren approaching. She looked longingly at her roadster parked across the street. So near and yet so far. She wiped nervous sweat from her brow with one hand, took a breath and stepped out onto the sidewalk…

"Which office is it?" questioned the burly cop as he pulled his revolver from its holster.

"Right there! I left the door open. She's locked in the inner office." Leading the way, the security guard entered the brightly lit office and pointed at the locked inner door, "I don't have a key for the inner door."

"You sure she's still in there?"

"She sure is! There's no way out of this office and I've been here the whole time. My partner stayed downstairs to let you in."

The two cops exchanged glances and a quick nod. The burly cop stepped up and rattled the locked door knob while his partner waved the guard back. Lowering his shoulder, the bigger cop gave a yell and charged the door. The lock tore out of the jam with a crack and the inner door flew open to crash against the wall. He nearly went down from his momentum but kept his feet, his partner crowding through close behind him.

Guns up, the two cops covered the empty room. The guard entered and looked around. His mouth fell open in surprise. The thin cop said, "Well, where is she?"

The security guard turned to them in shock, "She was here. I know it. She couldn't have gone anywhere…" He turned slowly to the open window. The two cops followed his glance. Holstering his revolver, the burly cop who had crashed the door walked around the desk and thrust his head out into the night air. He looked left and then right along the ledge. Finally, he looked downward half way expecting to see a body sprawled on the sidewalk below. He frowned as he scanned the street both ways. It was empty of traffic or pedestrians. All was quiet except for a suddenly silenced siren from around the front of the building. Whoever their mystery woman was she had vanished like the wind.

Back in her suite at the *Mark Hopkins*, Ellen sat on the edge of the bed and rubbed her sore feet. She sadly contemplated the ruined, silk stockings that lay on the floor. She shook her head thinking about the new found respect she had for all the hard working second story men out there. The work she normally did was a lot less dangerous than hanging off building ledges. She mentally resolved to stick to more ladylike burgling in the future. She wasn't a circus acrobat, after all.

She brightened though at the thought of the information she had gained. It now looked like she would have to make a short side trip on her trip back south. It was time to check up on the couple who had adopted Tammy's daughter.

Ellen checked out of her hotel very early on Sunday. By late morning she had traveled over to the Central Valley. At Hwy 99, she had turned north rather than south and half hour later was cruising through the city of Stockton. It was here that the Wagner's lived according to Isaac Cohen's files. It didn't take long to locate the modest house in a middle-class neighborhood. It turned out to be a well-kept little bungalow with a picket fence although Ellen noticed that the lawn needed mowing as she pulled to the curb in front of the house.

Getting out of the car she was considering her approach to the occupants when a young girl in a blue dress came running around the corner of the house, a small dog running alongside her barking and jumping. The child stopped and dropped to one knee, hugging the dog as it jumped up to lick her face.

The little girl looked to be nine or ten years old. She was blonde and had a clear, happy laugh. Ellen realized this must be Tammy's daughter and her heart went out to the young child. She stepped up to the picket fence and called out to the little girl, "What's your dog's name?"

The little girl looked up at Ellen and said proudly, "His name is Skipper!"

Ellen nodded knowingly, "That's a good name for a dog. And, what's yours?"

The girl answered, "Lizbeth. But Mommy calls me Beth."

"Hello, Beth. My name is Ellen. Are your Mommy and Daddy home?"

The little girl looked seriously at Ellen and answered, "My Daddy is sleeping. He doesn't feel good, but my Mom is home."

"Good, I 'd like to speak with her if I…"

Ellen didn't get to finish. The girl was already running for the front porch yelling out, "Mommmm! There's a lady who wants to talk to you," before she even reached the open front door. Ellen smiled, remembering how it was to be an excited little girl, and pushed open the wooden gate. She had nearly reached the front steps when a middle-aged woman pushed open the screen door and stepped out onto the covered porch. She was wiping her hands on a dish towel. Little Beth crowded out behind her, while Skipper scampered around under foot barking.

The woman's dress was worn but clean. Her dark blonde hair showed threads of gray sown through it. She would have been fairly attractive but there were dark circles under her eyes and she looked tired. Raising her voice to be heard over the barking, she pasted a weak smile on her face and asked, "Can I help you?"

Ellen stepped closer and asked, "Are you Mrs. Wagner?"

"Yes, I am."

Ellen stepped up onto the first step and held out her hand, "My name is Ellen Patrick and I have a lot to talk to you about."

Ellen set down her glass on the side table and stood up to go, "Thank you for the lemonade, Lisa." The sounds of Beth laughing and Skipper barking outside could be heard through the open windows of the living room.

Mrs. Wagner came forward and shook her hand, "Thank you for coming, Ellen. It's a remarkable story." She shook her head slightly. "John and I have often wondered about Elizabeth's real mother. Now we will have something to tell her when someday she asks."

Ellen nodded, "The story isn't over. It may have a happy ending yet. I'm sorry about your husband. I pray that he gets the help he needs." She turned to go but stopped, turned and put a hand on the older woman's shoulder. "You should tell Beth the truth soon. It will only be a bigger shock for her the longer you wait."

Lisa hesitated and nodded. "You're right. It'll take some preparation but it needs to be done."

The two women exited onto the porch. Beth came running across the overgrown front yard. To Ellen she asked, "Are you leaving?"

Ellen stepped down to meet her, "I'm afraid so. But I may be back sometime. Meanwhile, can you do something for me?" Beth nodded. "Good, I want you to take good care of your parents until I see you again. They love you very much. Can you do that for me?"

Beth agreed seriously. Ellen looked back at Lisa Wagner on the porch, "Take care of yourselves. I'll be in touch when I have more news." The older woman waved and called out, "Thank you," as Ellen turned to exit through the wooden gate.

Once again in her roadster across the street, Ellen fired up the powerful engine. She glanced out the side and saw mother and daughter waving to her from the porch. Ellen waved back a she let in the clutch and pulled away from the curb.

She was busy for several minutes navigating city traffic but once on the highway headed south, she had time to get angry. The Wagner's were decent folk and good parents to Tammy's daughter but they had fallen on hard times. The company Mr. Wagner had worked for had been hit hard by the depression. Layoffs had left the workers short-handed. With everyone trying to do too much work there had been an accident and Mr. Walker had injured his back. Worker's compensation benefits had been exhausted, quickly followed by their savings. But that money had run out and more was needed. The family was at risk of losing their home.

Ellen had accomplished her mission. She had located Tammy's daughter and just in time it seemed. Now that daughter and her new family were threatened. Ellen was not going to let this good family be destroyed. Someone was going to make this right. She and her masked alter ego would see to it.

After a long trip home, Ellen had gotten to bed late. But she was still up early enough the next morning to present herself at Whitaker campaign headquarters to start her new volunteer job. After all, she wanted to make a good impression.

Fred Harris was there to get her started. He was somewhat grumpy until Ellen presented him with a donation of ten dollars. Her personal contribution to the Assemblyman's re-election she told him with a smile. It's amazing how someone's disposition could be improved with money in their hands.

Fred put her to work addressing and stuffing envelopes. The office was busy with several other, mostly young people busy with various campaign activities. The phones rang often and people came and went. Ellen exchanged a friendly word with him when Nathan Whitaker arrived. He paused by the table she was working at to thank her and flirt a bit. Ellen smiled and flirted back. This was all part of her plan and she was pleased.

At noon, Ellen and a few of her fellow volunteers went down the street to a diner for lunch. There she caught up on the office gossip. A friendly young volunteer named Betty confirmed Ellen's suspicions when she warned Ellen to be careful of the Assemblyman. He was very friendly with the female staff and prone to get very 'handsy' when no one was looking. Betty, who stated she had a very jealous boyfriend, of course claimed to be innocent of any hanky-panky herself. Interestingly, she told Ellen to be especially wary of Mrs. Whitaker who kept a close eye on her candidate husband and a suspicious eye on the female office workers.

At the end of the day Ellen was glad to head back to her Wilshire apartment and put her feet up. She absently sucked on a finger where an annoying paper cut hurt like the dickens. She was glad she didn't have to do this kind of work for a living. Still, she was near Nathan Whitaker and learning a lot.

Over the next few days Ellen learned even more. She answered telephones, stuffed envelopes, even tacked up election flyers on telephone poles around the district one day with Betty and a volunteer name Gus. She was unpacking a box of posters and thinking of lunch when Whitaker stepped up to her. She saw him often and exchanged pleasantries with him but he had been nothing but correct with her. Today, he smiled and asked, "Well Ellen, how are you finding it here. Are we keeping you busy?"

"Oh yes, Mr. Whitaker. It's exciting to be her helping your re-election. And, yes I've been very busy."

"Yes, there's always lots to do a round a campaign headquarters. Fred tells me you're fitting in just fine. I've been watching too and I can see that you're a hard worker. It makes me proud to represent such fine people in my district."

"Why, thank you, Mr. Whitaker. That's high praise."

"Call me, Nathan. Why don't you let me take you to lunch to show you my thanks?" Whitaker waved his hand. Ellen looked around saw people grabbing their jackets and purses. Looking up at the clock on the wall she saw that it was coming up on noon, "Why, it's lunch time! I was so busy I lost track of time." Ellen tried to look innocent as she looked Whitaker in the eye, "I am hungry, though."

"Good. Grab your purse, I'm buying."

Ellen did just that. Moments later she was on the sidewalk with Whitaker. He took her elbow and gently steered her toward a new Buick parked at the curb just down the street. Ellen pretended surprise, "Aren't we going to the diner? Everyone should be there."

"As you say, the place will be busy. I have some place else in mind. It's not far and very quiet. The food's good as well."

"Okay, that sounds good."

In the Buick Whitaker quickly steered them to a small restaurant several blocks away. As he had said it was quiet. The staff seemed to know him and they quickly showed the couple to a booth near the rear of the restaurant. Once seated, they quickly ordered and while they waited Whitaker tried to get to know Ellen, "Tell me about yourself, Ellen."

"Well, I live here in town with my mother. I worked as secretary downtown for a while but the company I worked for went bankrupt. So, I moved back here. That's why I have time to volunteer for you. I'm looking around for something new but jobs are scarce. You know how it is."

Whitaker concurred. "Times are hard. That's why it's so important I am re-elected so I can continue to help people."

Or so you don't have to get a real job, thought Ellen as she listened to Whitaker talk. He was smooth. She had to give him credit. He seemed genuinely interested in Ellen. He asked all the right questions and seemed sincere about getting to know her. Fortunately, she knew better. Whitaker wasn't the first lady's man she had dealt with. Cads like him had tried to seduce her before. She knew what to look for and how to play them like hooked trout.

Ellen pasted a look of hero worship on her face. "It must be wonderful at the state capital making all those laws and helping all those people."

Whitaker swelled up at the praise. Trying to sound modest he launched into a story, "Well, it is very rewarding to..."

After lunch, as she worked answering phones, Ellen thought how easily it was to manipulate self-important men like Whitaker. Just turn the questions back on them. She had yet to meet a politician who didn't like talking about himself.

Late that night, a tall woman with a black cloak watched the street in front of the campaign headquarters from a darkened alley. The street was empty. She stepped out of the alley and glided along the sidewalk to the front door of the headquarters. Glancing left, then right before pulling out her trusty lock pick, she went to work. A minute later she was closing the front door behind her. Turning the lock, she waited a few moments for her eyes to adjust to the darkness, then made her way carefully across the open front area to the rear offices.

Inside Whitaker's private office she closed the door and flashed a small penlight around. Against one wall were three file cabinets. Although doubtful, she started searching there to be thorough. Ten minutes later she had found nothing, as she had suspected and turned to the desk. It was locked but the simple lock yielded quickly.

The desk held mostly routine office supplies and correspondence. Although one folder contained correspondence with several obviously wealthy campaign donors. Nothing illegal but she raised an eyebrow at the amounts discussed as well as the legislation that these donors expected for their money. More interesting was the contents of the top right-hand drawer. The loaded, thirty-two caliber revolver drew her attention but not as much as the personal check book she found. Leafing through it, showed nothing overtly illegal but it did show the Whitakers' spent a lot of money and apparently lived very well.

This was interesting but was certainly not damning. The contents of the lower right-hand drawer were more promising. Here the Domino Lady found the campaign's ledgers. Assuring herself that the door to the office was closed she seated herself at the Assemblyman's desk and turned on the small desk lamp. Opening the first ledger she went to work.

As Ellen Patrick, Domino Lady had spent four years at UC Berkeley gaining a fine education. While not a finance or accounting major she had taken courses in math and business basics. She had also learned much about running businesses both large and small in her work crusading against corruption. She called up what knowledge she had and went to work.

Two hours later she closed the ledger, turned off the lamp and leaned back in Whitaker's comfortable office chair. In the dark she rested her eyes and thought about what she had found out.

While Whitaker was taking in a surprising amount of money from wealthy donors most of it seemed on the up and up. She recognized most of the names and or companies involved as legitimate businesses. Although there were a couple of names, she did want to double check. Reluctantly, she was forced to admit that Whitaker was probably not taking in any organized crime money. That was not to say that his donors would not expect their pet Assemblyman to vote the way they expected when he returned to the legislature in Sacramento. No, they most certainly would have their hands out when the time came.

No, it seemed that Whitaker was no worse than any other politician who was afraid of being turned out of office and forced to get real job. She had hoped for decisive evidence of illegal activities.

Of more interest was his personal life. While going through the ledgers Domino Lady had found an interesting pattern. Whitaker would from time to time make large personal withdrawals for his campaign fund. These would have no reasons listed but simple were listed as 'personal.' Interestingly, these matched deposits into his personal checking account. More interestingly, the campaign ledgers often showed large donations in the days and weeks after these withdrawals. She had double checked the personal correspondence file she had found earlier and found that these deposits tallied with appeals Whitaker made to some of his most dependable donors.

Domino Lady frowned in the dark. She was no lawyer. She knew little about campaign laws. While it was apparent that Whitaker and his wife were using the campaign as their personal bank, making withdraws to finance their no doubt fine lifestyle. She had no idea if this was illegal or just unethical. Still, she was sure this was just the handle she needed to manipulate the assemblyman. Now the decision was how to use it.

The black cloaked figure exited the building as quietly, as she had entered. Before she did, she left one of her black calling cards with the words, *Compliments of the Domino Lady* buried deep at the bottom of the lower drawer. She was confident that it would not be found until far after matters would be decided. Minutes later she was in her roadster driving through the deserted early morning streets.

Not wanting to draw attention to herself Ellen continued working at the campaign headquarters for the next few days. The office was busy and Whitaker was his usual ingratiating self. He went out of his way to be friendly to Ellen, even taking her to lunch once again. She smiled and pretended interest in his flattering remarks. He made it obvious that he was interested in a more personal relationship with her. She endured his advances with smiles and returned them with flirtations of her own.

On the third day after her midnight foray to headquarters, she was very interested in Whitaker's actions. He came in late and seemed rattled. He had a quick and confidential conversation with his manager Harris before leaving hurriedly with both his checkbook and the campaign ledgers. Ellen smiled to herself as she continued addressing envelopes, thinking back to the Domino Lady's visit with Whitaker the night before.

Whitaker had worked late at headquarters. By the time he locked up, the street was dark and deserted. His car was parked just down the street opposite a narrow opening between two buildings that led to the alley behind the row of buildings. He unlocked the passenger door and tossed in his briefcase. As he slammed the door, Domino Lady glided out of the narrow passageway leading to the alley and slid up behind Whitaker. She jammed her little automatic up under his hat against his neck and whispered through the scarf across her face, "Don't move!"

Whitaker raised his hands slowly out from his sides, "Don't shoot! You can have my wall…Oww!" His voice cut off as he grabbed for his neck. Withdrawing the syringe and stepping back, she watched the politician glance around at her before his eyes rolled up in his head and he crumpled to the dark sidewalk. Picking up his key ring, Domino Lady grabbed the unconscious man under

Domino Lady frowned in the dark.

his shoulders and dragged him twenty feet along the sidewalk to the front of his campaign headquarters, grunting with the effort.

It took only moments more to unlock the front door and drag Whitaker's limp form into the building. With the door safely locked she pulled a pocket flash from a pocket in her black cape and went to work.

An hour later Whitaker groaned and shook his head. The effort hurt and he groaned in pain. He tried to reach for his head but found his hand would not move. That brought him awake fighting the cobwebs that covered his thoughts. He managed to open his eyes but saw nothing that made sense. He was in darkness with a light somewhere behind him. A huge shadow loomed in front of him.

Suddenly a gloved hand appeared from over his shoulder and dashed a glass of water in his face. The assemblyman spluttered and spit. He blinked water out of his eyes and his vision cleared. He realized he was seated in a chair looking at a wall dominated by a huge poster of his own smiling face over the words, "Re-elect Whitaker for State Assembly!" The room was dark with only one source of light directly behind him. More alarmingly, his hands were bound to the arms of the wheeled office chair.

A muffled woman's voice spoke from behind him, "Glad to see you're awake and alert, Assemblyman. We have a lot to talk about."

Whitaker gulped and attempted to keep his voice calm, "I don't know what you want but it's not…"

"I'll do the talking. Just keep quiet and listen. I know a lot about you Whitaker. I've been watching you for a long time and looking for you for far longer. You may think you've forgotten about the past but it hasn't forgotten about you. Now it's time to pay up."

The calm, matter of fact voice chilled Whitaker to the bone. He wasn't sure what was going on but he was sure he was in trouble. He would have to tread carefully, "Uh…look. We can talk this over. Whatever you want, I'm sure we can work something out.

"Well, that's an interesting response, Assemblyman. What do you think it's about? All those questionable campaign donations or the fact that you use your campaign fund as a personal piggy bank to be tapped whenever you feel the need. Or maybe it's about something a lot farther back in your sordid past."

A chill ran down Whitakers spine that had nothing to do with the water running down his collar. Various possibilities tumble through his mind. Who was this and how did they know so much? He licked his lips and spoke carefully, "I don't know what you're talk…"

"Shut up! Listen carefully." There was a long pause before the mysterious woman asked, "Do you remember back to what you were doing ten years ago, Counselor? You were a young lawyer working in northern California, Remember?"

Caught off guard Whitaker was confused, "What's that got to do with anything?"

"Oh, it's got everything to do with everything. Let me refresh your memory. You were a lawyer who had a young neighbor girl who babysat for you and your wife. Do you remember her?"

Whitaker stiffened. He drew in a quick breath, licked his lips and tried to answer calmly. "Uh, that was along time ago. My wife and I moved around and we had several baby sitters."

"Oh. That's interesting. Did you seduce all of them? Did you manage to get all of them pregnant?"

Whitaker froze. He tried to answer but his mouth was suddenly dry as if filled with sand. He swallowed, licked his lips and managed to stutter out, "Uhhh. I uh, don't know what you mean."

"It doesn't matter. I know everything I need to know. Everything important that is." There was the slightest pause then the voice continued in an angry hiss, "I know how you bought your way out of that scandal. A pressured adoption, confidentiality agreements, and you walk away clean. But others remember." Whitaker's heart was beating hard in his chest. He twisted his wrists against the cords that tied him to the chair. He was painfully aware that he was helpless. There was no one within shouting distance. He was bound to the chair and whoever this woman was, she was clearly dangerous.

The voice continued, "Speaking of people knowing, does your wife know? Does she know about your other little romances? Of course, she knows! I know she even helped you cover up your unknown child and pay off her mother. Why she stays with you is beyond me?"

There was pause and Whitaker wanted to say something but had no idea what would satisfy this woman. He licked his lips. Could it be? No! Why would she come after him now and how did she know? Those records were all confidential.

The woman continued, "I know what a lady's man you think you are. Why, I'll even bet that if I dig a little deeper, I'll find a lot of other sordid affairs in your past. I know how men like you are."

Whitaker again licked his lips. There was only one thing to do. He spoke carefully, "What do you want?"

"What do I want? I want a little justice for that sixteen-year-old girl. You know, the one whose life you ruined. The one who felt guilty and blamed herself for years. The one you walked away from after you got what you wanted and left her pregnant!" There was a pause, "Well, the time has come to pay up for your crimes, Nathan. You've skated for too long. So, I want twenty thousand dollars. Otherwise, all this information is going directly to your rival. I'm sure he would love to have a nice pre-election scandal to throw at you."

Whitaker was so shocked he couldn't reply for a second, when he found his voice, he croaked out, "Twenty thousand! I don't have that kind of money!"

"Sure you do. I've seen your house. I know how nicely you live. You have plenty of money and access to even more."

"What do you mean?"

"I mean, I know how you're tapping your campaign fund for personal use. And, that's something else. I don't know much about campaign laws but I'm pretty sure that the laws covering embezzling probably apply here. One way or another the DA will be very interested in how you run your campaign. Not to mention the newspapers and your worthy opponent. So, you better go home and tap your piggy bank, make some withdrawals or do whatever it takes to get the money I want or you're going to be more famous than even a photo hungry politician would want to be."

After a quick thinking pause, Whitaker choked out, "I'll need some time."

"Okay, you have twenty-four hours. I want the money by tomorrow night."

"What! That's impossible!"

"Oh, I don't think so. I have every confidence that you can be very creative when it comes to finances." The Domino Lady stepped back toward the door to Whitakers' office. Her hand on the door, she added, "Tomorrow night. Here. Midnight. Twenty thousand in small bills or you're going to be famous all-over Southern California."

She turned, opened the door and stepped through. As she was about to close it, Whitaker spoke over his shoulder, "Look, I'm sorry about...about back then. I didn't mean to hurt uh, you or anyone."

Caught off guard but not surprised at Whitaker's assumption. She answered, "It's a little late, I'm afraid." Closing the door softly she disappeared into the shadows.

"I'm sorry, Barb." Whitaker held his hands up palm out. "It's not my fault. I don't know how this woman knows what she knows. But it means that..."

The tall, thin brunette woman pointed a well-manicured, accusing finger at her husband, "I know what it means! It means that little skirt is back! And, it

is your fault! If you could keep it in your pants for more than five minutes at a stretch we wouldn't be in this mess! And, don't try to look innocent! You're not any good at it. This isn't the first time you've been caught with your pants down!"

Whitaker quailed before his wife's temper. Holding up a hand he spoke gently attempting to mollify the angry woman, "Dear, it's not like that. I may have made some mistakes in the past but that's all behi…"

"Don't give me that horse crap! I've heard about the new girl down at headquarters! And, how you've been romancing her! I'm getting sick of this. If we weren't in the middle of an election, I'd…" She broke off and stalked across the room to a side table. There she grabbed up a bottle and poured a healthy dose of golden-brown liquid into a glass. She took a sip and thought a moment before saying, "Okay, we're going to have to buy this woman off. It's a pain in the ass but we've got to keep her quiet."

"But Barb, we don't have enough money on hand and by tomorrow…"

"Then we use the campaign's money. Go to the bank tomorrow and we'll figure out how to juggle the books later." She paused for a moment to take a long drink from her glass before adding, "With a little luck we can come out of this on top. Here's what we're going to do. . ."

The Domino Lady smiled as she stood in the shadows of the broom closet with the door open. She had been so pleased to see how rattled Whitaker had seemed today. She had found herself whistling as she worked in the office the rest of the day. Now, certain that Whitaker would bring the money she waited patiently. She was sure the frightened politician would pay but come early to the rendezvous just to be safe. She stretched in the darkness to stay loose. She couldn't see her watch in the darkness but she knew it must be getting close to midnight.

Moments later a soft scratching sound came to her ears. She reached out and pulled the door nearly closed. With her automatic in one hand, she leaned to the crack and listened. She heard a lock turn and a door open. A single set of footsteps crossed the room. Dim light suddenly came from across the main office. So, Whitaker had come alone. Good. But something about the steps bothered her.

Pushing the closet door silently open, Domino Lady ghosted across the darkened main office toward the lit doorway leading to Whitaker's office. She could hear someone inside moving about.

Her automatic at her side, Domino Lady stepped into the doorway. A well-dressed woman stood next to the desk, a small, open valise in front of her.

Sensing movement, she looked up and directly into the eyes of the masked woman in front of her. They were both startled for an instant. Whitaker's wife, no doubt, because of the mask, cape and gun. The Domino Lady because she had certainly not expected a woman.

Quickly recovering, Domino Lady spoke first, "I guess your husband wasn't man enough to bring the money himself."

Barb Whitaker sneered, "I'm cleaning up his messes, as usual. You don't think we don't know you're that little dame that lived up the street, back for a little payoff. You don't think that mask will hide who you are, do you?"

Domino Lady was secretly amused at the mistaken identity but she kept her voice neutral as she pointed with her free hand at the desk. "Is that the money?"

Whitaker reached into the valise and lifted out a wrapped bundle of green backs. Domino Lady stepped forward gesturing with her hand, "Good. I'll just be on my way, then."

"Not so fast. I want the name of the family who adopted the child."

Surprised Domino Lady stopped and said, "I don't think so. The child may be your husband's but it is safe and happy now."

The woman shook her head. "No name. No money." She dropped the cash back into the bag and reached out to latch the bag closed. Instead, her hand darted inside and came out with a pistol.

Surprised, Domino Lady lunged forward. She knocked the woman's arm upward as Whitaker squeezed off a shot. The slug went somewhere past the masked woman's shoulder. Domino Lady dropped her own pistol to the floor and wrapped both hands around Whitaker's gun arm. She twisted in opposite directions. Whitaker screamed and dropped her gun in turn. She then clawed at the masked woman's face. Domino Lady fended the furious woman off with her right elbow. She felt a sharp pain in her shin as Whitaker kicked outward.

Stepping quickly back, she jerked Whitaker forward. Off balance, the woman's right arm stretched outward, Domino Lady spun her around bending the now cursing woman's arm up in a hammer lock.

Domino Lady then shoved the Whitaker forward to the desk and bent her over it. Finally, in control, she leaned forward, pinning her opponent down as she hiked her long dress up to reach underneath it.

Whitaker screamed, "You bitch! This is blackmail, you won't get away with it. We can find you!"

Domino Lady laughed. "Who will you be looking for," just before she plunged the syringe into Mrs. Whitaker's neck? She held her down until the woman's struggles stopped and she passed out.

Taking a deep breath, Domino Lady looked around. The single shot seemed to have drawn no attention. Quickly she gathered her automatic and syringe.

She then pulled enough cash out of the bag to do a rough count. Twenty thousand as promised. She set half aside and scattered the rest across the desk. She then picked up the telephone and clicked the lever a few times until a woman answered, "Operator."

"Operator, get me the police. It's an emergency."

"One moment, please."

In the minute it took for the police to answer, she looked over the woman sprawled across the desk. It was clear to her who wore the pants in the Whitaker family. Whitaker was just another self-centered politician with his hand out. She was much more the dangerous of the two. Perhaps what they said about the female of the species being more dangerous than the male was true. Something to remember.

A voice came on the line, "Sergeant Parsons. What's the emergency?"

Putting a bit of excitement in her voice, the masked woman, spoke quickly, "I was driving past the Whitaker campaign headquarters on *Crenshaw* when I heard gunfire from inside. Lots of shots! You better come quick!"

"Alright, ma'am. Calm down. Whitaker campaign headquarters on Crenshaw. We're coming. Now, tell me what your name is."

Domino Lady quickly hung up the phone. She picked up Whitaker's automatic in her gloved hands and fired twice into the walls. She then pulled Whitaker down onto the floor arranging her limbs in as natural a position as possible. She then pressed the gun into Whitaker's limp right hand. Lastly, she opened the sleeping woman's purse and slipped a black business card with the words *Compliments of the Domino Lady* written in white on it into the purse and snapped it shut. Picking up the stack of money, she walked to the door and looked back. An unconscious woman with a gun in her hand, bullets fired and money scattered all over the desk. This would all be very interesting for the police. She smiled thinking of all the awkward questions that Mrs. Whitaker would be soon answering.

As she exited the street door she flipped on the overhead lights. Leaving the door wide open she strolled casually to the narrow alley mouth and disappeared into the darkness.

"Look into it. I'm sure you'll find an interesting story there," Ellen spoke into the phone.

As the voice on the other end of the line said, "But, who are..." she again hung up. Thinking that her phone manners sometimes left something to be desired she shook her head. Glancing down at the folded back copy of this morning's *Times*, she smiled at the headline. "Candidate and wife questioned in mysterious shooting."

Whitaker and his wife had made the news. After reading the article, Ellen had made a call to the *Times* reporter whose byline appeared at the top of the article. She had given him an earful of information on Whitaker's campaign machinations, then hinted of past sexual abuses that had been covered up. She was sure that a thorough investigation would turn up lots of dirt on the Assemblyman. In any event, his political career would be over.

A day later, Ellen was in her roadster driving through the sunny but crowded streets of Hollywood. She was headed north on a trip. First though, she had a stop to make. Finding a parking space near a post office, she left the car and walked a block to stand in line at the busy branch office, a small package under her arm. As she waited, she glanced down at the package. It was addressed to a Catholic orphanage here in Southern California. It contained a good sized, anonymous, cash donation; courtesy of the Whitakers. She hoped that Tammy would be pleased at this gesture.

Back on the road, she headed north through the San Fernando Valley and over the mountains toward the Central Valley. Stockton would be her first stop. The money she had would be a lot of help for the Wagners. As she drove, she found herself looking forward to seeing the happy child Beth again. Ellen had never thought a lot about motherhood. Her dangerous life style kept thoughts of marriage and motherhood at bay. But who knew; someday she might have a daughter much like Tammy's beautiful little girl? The thought gave her pause. Dealing with corrupt officials and crooked business men wasn't good training for motherhood. Raising a daughter was something else entirely. Could she do something like that? Suddenly the 'terror of California corruption' was filled with self-doubts. What kind of mother would she make? That was a lot of responsibility.

Shaking her head, she thought, "Well, there's plenty of time for all that later." Meanwhile Stockton and maybe...a quick side trip to San Francisco were ahead of her. She laughed gaily and pressed down on the accelerator.

The End

BEHIND THE MASK

*Y*ou know, after you've written a series character for a while, people sometimes ask if you're getting bored writing her or him. Well, this will be my fifth or possibly sixth (depending on schedules) published Domino Lady story and I have not gotten bored yet. There's a lot to be said for writing a series character; for me the writing gets easier. After all, I know the character. I don't have to start fresh with each new story. After a while, I almost instinctively know how she'll react in a given situation. Feeling relaxed with Domino Lady has made writing her adventures both easy and fun.

Over the years I have been chronicling her adventures, I have been surprised by how easily ideas for her adventures came to me. I worried once or twice that I might run out of ideas for stories starring the beautiful, masked adventuress but that doesn't seem to have happened yet. And with luck won't happen any time soon. I firmly believe there are still lots of Domino Lady tales to be told.

Being able to pick and choose, at a given time, which stories about a character I get to write is a luxury I don't often have. With several story ideas ready to go, I decided to show a different side to California's lovely masked avenger. In this story, she is thrust into situations where things don't go necessarily as planned. She has to think fast and stretch her physical abilities a bit. After all, not all of even Domino Lady's well-planned forays can be expected to go perfectly.

Also, we all think of Ellen Patrick/Domino Lady as a carefree, devil-may-care adventuress; and she is. But she is also a young woman who may have dreams of love and family as many of us do. I decided to open this door and show a little of her more sensitive side.

All this means that in this story you will see a little more of Ellen Patrick and a little bit less of her masked alter ego. Not necessarily a bad thing. Whether wearing her domino mask or not, here she is at her best; infiltrating, manipulating and confounding her corrupt and crooked foes.

I ended up doing a good bit of research for this story. That kind of work is easy, though. As a former history major, I like nothing more than digging into local California history or researching hit songs from the 1930s. Details are important and good research is crucial for those. Whether it is the proper Catholic Parrish for Santa Barbara in 1932 or street locations in Inglewood.

The writing itself went fast through the first half of the story. Then I got distracted. First by a brand-new Domino Lady story that suddenly popped into my mind and demanded to be outlined immediately. Then by another

41

writing opportunity that came out of nowhere and had to be addressed right then and there.

So, after an intermission of a few weeks, I reacquainted myself with *The Domino Lady's Daughter* and finished it in a week. Revisions were surprisingly few. Mostly revising a few awkward conversations (Who wrote this stuff?).

In the end I am quite happy with *The Domino Lady's Daughter*. It is a little bit different but I think fans will enjoy a fresh look at our lovely masked avenger's life. I hope all of you readers agree.

Needless to say, my next Domino Lady story is outlined and ready to go. As long as Airship 27 continues to publish her adventures, I hope to be there with new stories. See you next time.

GENE MOYERS - studied European and Medieval history at the University of Oregon. He is also a U.S. Army veteran. He worked in the high-tech industry for some time and is also a licensed massage therapist.

An avid military gamer and role player, his favorite game was *Daredevils* a pulp based roleplaying game set in the 1930s. His love affair with the 1930s and pulps in particular stem from his first time reading a *Shadow* novel as a boy. Although interested in writing since a teen he did not turn to serious writing until 2000.

He is the co-author of *GURPS Crusades* published by Steve Jackson Games. He has written several stories for Airship 27 including stories published in all of the *Purple Scar volumes,* all of the *Domino Lady volumes, Mystery Men and Women vol.5, The Phantom Detective vol.1, Moon Man vol. 2, Dan Fowler vol.3* and *The Legends of New Pulp Fiction.* He has also written a story published in *Alternative Air Adventures* for Pro Se Publications and one published in *I.V Frost Scientific Detective* for Moonstone Books.

When not working on various new pulp projects, he is busy writing alternate history stories or horror adventures for his occult investigator, the *Dream Master.* Safe from Covid-19 in his hidden sanctum deep in the forests of the Great Northwest, Gene currently continues writing, carefully watched over by his wife and two lazy dogs.

THE DOMINO LADY AND THE FABERGÉ EGG

By George Tackes

Ellen Patrick knew the nearly four-inch jeweled artifact would fit nicely nestled within the fleshy canyon of her ample cleavage covered only by the gown's flimsy garnet bodice. She could waltz right out of the University Library hall past the armed security smuggling the fabulous Imperial Russian heirloom and no one would be the wiser. However, she mused that a woman's chest is usually the place at which most men tend to first glance when encountering the opposite sex.

Certainly, no gentlemen would search there for it. But not all men are gentlemen, she reflected.

A dazzling smile curved across her crimson lips emphasizing the pearly whiteness of her teeth. Her moist lipstick matched perfectly with the scarlet satin one-shoulder full-length evening gown. The lissome socialite dressed exquisitely for this elegant affair at her alma mater, University of California, Berkeley.

A few paces away stood Gregorio Canning and his wife, Raquel, another U. of C. alumna. They hosted this elaborate reception of cocktails and hors d'oeuvres to unveil their prized acquisition to be on temporary loan to the University. The gray-haired millionaire sported a classic black tuxedo and the auburn-haired, vulpine-faced millionairess graced a silver ball gown detailed with black bead and lace work.

Ellen glimpsed at them and then back to the formerly "lost" Fabergé Egg perched on a thin silver wire throne on top of a Doric column pedestal. A crystal glass dome lay at its base. The singular exhibition flaunted itself like a peninsula surrounded by red velvet ropes and chrome stanchions harbored within the cavernous main hall of the University Library.

Selected staff, influential alumni, and prestigious donors were honored to attend the special invite-only intimate gathering to exhibit the opulent 1909 Fabergé Egg. The recently discovered Alexander III Commemorative Easter Egg was an ovoid-shaped, diamond encrusted, gold-latticed, white-enamel piece of art rumored to hide a miniature bust of the Russian emperor inside. The renowned Russian jeweler, Peter Carl Fabergé, designed it specifically for Emperor Nicholas II of Russia as an Easter present for his mother.

43

The fabled history of the Egg was irrelevant to Ellen. As the Domino Lady, she was only interested in its monetary value and how to de-throne it from its perch.

Ellen held the multiple distinctions of being not only a University of California alumna and a generous donor but a sorority sister of Raquel Landis, now Canning. So the fact that she would rate such an elite invitation was presupposed.

Seeing Raquel would be a delight, of course, but reuniting with their fellow Alpha Phi Beta sorority sister, Lisa Brown, was the clincher, the deciding factor to attend this prestigious and somewhat pompous affair. Also, the exhibition offered the Domino Lady the opportunity to discretely reconnoiter the valuable Egg and its security precautions.

Prestigious and pompous functions were Raquel's forte now. Raquel succeeded in her life's goal – earn a business administrative degree and then marry a wealthy executive. At one time, she harbored a bit of envy toward Ellen's money and status but now her wealth and status superseded Ellen's. Still she behaved graciously about it.

Ellen, on the other hand, couldn't care less.

Gregorio, however, admired Ellen's shapely leg peeking out of the side slit in her gown covering her svelte body like red wet paint.

Raquel stabbed her husband in his ribs with her elbow. Then she reached out to Ellen with both arms stretched but did not move from her husband's side.

Ellen sashayed over to the stationary hostess. She and Raquel greeted each other with the appropriate arm hug and kiss on the cheek.

But when Lisa walked into the room, they both squealed with delight at the friendly face. They rushed over to the tall woman in the beige tapered slack suit.

All three hugged and giggled as if they were co-eds once again. Lisa, a couple of years older, served as a surrogate big sister to both of them.

"You look wonderful. What're you up to now?" Ellen asked.

"Our lovely Lisa is now Professor Elizabeth Brown of the History Department at the University of California, Berkeley!" Raquel bragged.

"Professor Elizabeth Brown, I like that!" Ellen repeated with pride.

"It's Lisa, you twits! And, don't forget the P, H and D!"

The three gabbed away and caught up as Gregorio sauntered up to join the chattering trio.

"Still, fencing?" Ellen asked.

"Fencing?" Gregorio interrupted.

Ellen linked her arm with Lisa's. "Our Wonderful Miss Lisa was part of the

1932 Olympics. The Women's Fencing Team."

"Not a team. Women only compete in the individual foil event," Lisa chuckled modestly.

"Very impressive," Gregorio nodded.

"I didn't make it to the round robin," Lisa clarified.

"Still, you must be in very impressive shape to compete," Gregorio leered. Raquel nudged him and emitted a wilting squint with her amber eyes.

"Ever since I saw Douglas Fairbanks swordfight in 'The Mark of Zorro,' I was in love. With the sword, not Douglas Fairbanks," she joked.

Everyone let out a hearty laugh.

"It's also the source of her fascination with the history of California, her academic specialty, or so the tale goes," a nearby young brunette sighed drolly.

"Let me introduce my invaluable teaching assistant, Miss Christina Canfield. Her thesis focuses on the jewelry of Russian royalty. She's here to observe firsthand an actual Fabergé Egg. In fact, she designed the décor in the security alcove."

Despite being draped in a simple dark green evening tea swing dress, Christina presented herself as a haughty young collegiate with an air of superiority.

"Call me Tina, if you please," she sighed again in an attempt to be amiable.

Ellen noted a touch of a Midwestern accent.

"From Chicago?"

"Yes." Tina raised an eyebrow suspiciously as she assessed the socialite in the daring scarlet evening gown.

"Good ear, Ellen. You might take note. Naturally Tina's fluent in Russian," Lisa said.

To emphasize the fact, Tina said, "Privet, napyshchennaya zadnitsa."

Smiling, Ellen nodded her blonde head and replied, with "Privet ty vysokomernaya suka."

Tina's face froze. Her eyes squinched intensely. A sincere smile broke across her face. "I like you. I think we will be friends."

Ellen knew instinctively she liked this woman too, a kindred spirit.

"When I was a student, not too long ago, my field of study was foreign languages, my dear."

The Canning's Chinese servant, not surprisingly wearing a white Tangshan jacket with a straight collar, arrived at Gregorio's right side holding a silver serving tray with two martinis for the couple. He submissively bowed his head as Gregorio lifted the cocktails with each hand and presented one to his wife.

Ellen greeted the servant in Mandarin Chinese. He responded with a wide-eyed look of stark terror.

Gregorio interjected. "I'm afraid Kai is mute. And as I'm sure you're aware, China is notorious for its multitude of Chinese dialects. You may not be speaking in the one from the remote region where he's from. He does understand some English. Would you like him to fetch you something to drink?"

Kai managed a weak smile and nodded sharply toward Ellen. His black hair plastered down so it did not move.

"No, thank you," she said to Gregorio and then in a louder, slower manner repeated the same to Kai. Kai bowed and turned to Gregorio.

"That's all for this evening, Kai. You may return to our rooms," Gregorio commanded with a tilt of his head.

"We're staying at the President's House," Raquel bragged a bit.

"Ooo, the University president's humble abode. Impressive, Raquel," Ellen raved.

Raquel beamed.

"Would you please excuse me? I'd like to take a closer look at the object d'arte," Tina said in a warmer and humbler tone.

"I'd be honored to give you a personal viewing and let these girls catch up," Gregorio offered.

Presenting his arm and ignoring the glare from his wife, Gregorio escorted Tina to the Fabergé Egg. He even allowed her to hold it and lift the gold-latticed cap to examine the golden miniature bust inside. She gingerly cradled the Egg and barely breathed on it as if a tiny puff might irreparably tarnish it.

The three former sorority sisters chatted away.

"He's quite a bit older than you, isn't he?" Lisa asked shyly.

"Family trait, I suppose. Remember my older cousin, Nora?"

"Lanky brunette with the wicked jaw?" Ellen said searching her memory.

"Yes. Married a Greek from out East somewhere. Fifteen years her senior. Gregorio's only a dozen or so older than me," Raquel admitted proudly as if this one-upped her cousin somehow. He was actually twenty years older than her.

Ellen couldn't help but enjoy the snarky gossip but her focus repeatedly drifted back to the Fabergé Egg. She knew attaining such an artifact couldn't have been managed by any legal means or without paying off corrupt officials along the way to import or smuggle it through international customs into the United States.

During Raquel and Gregorio's wedding (which occurred within a year after divorcing his first wife), Ellen learned of some unscrupulous dealings in the groom's past from some older men trying to impress her. Stodgy, old men think regaling tales of daring business deals present a charming, dark side to beautiful young damsels. She remained aloof to such bluster, but did take note of a couple corrupt politicians among the wedding guests. Further casual wedding scuttlebutt revealed Gregorio's business dealings incorporated dubious and discreet enterprises, but nothing wholly illegal, just shady. Ellen knew that loaning the Fabergé Egg to the University to display and study was an obvious attempt to publicly legitimize ownership of it. The Egg had to have been obtained unlawfully. Ellen instinctively knew it.

Without providing details, Gregorio and Raquel claimed the Fabergé Egg came into their possession by a fluke, a mere twist of fate, during a business trip abroad. Gregorio claimed he stumbled onto it and Raquel gushed that it "sort of" fell into their laps. Both saw obtaining the Egg as a way to honor Gregorio's Russian heritage. Raquel couldn't resist its divine beauty and the financial prestige it symbolized.

In between gossiping with Raquel and Lisa, Ellen anticipated the theft-proof obstacles. The Fabergé Egg would remain stored and secured within the main library which housed all of the University's fragile and valuable collections. Burglar alarms and locks and security patrols were expected. A further complication included a vault-like alcove for the Egg specially constructed in the middle of the Doe Memorial Library that was in the middle of the Berkeley campus, not near any road for an easy getaway.

Mentally, Ellen engineered various schemes on how the Domino Lady could relieve the Cannings of their ill-gotten Egg.

During the reception, she intimately familiarized herself with the Library's security systems by flirtations and innocent banter with the University's chief security officer, also an honored guest. Decked out in full turquoise uniform with epaulets and peaked police cap, he was very impressed with his position and knowledge of security management. All of which he shared in fine detail with Ellen to thrill her with his brilliance. He supplied all the necessary information she required to counter every security measures. His wife eventually ended their conversation.

Satisfied with the formulation of a well-devised plan, Ellen expected to enjoy the rest of the evening drinking, smoking, and socializing. Her concept of socializing entailed additional flirting with several single men in attendance. Now that the Fabergé Egg was no longer her focus, a certain tall, dark-haired male specimen attracted her attention. He was speaking with the self-important chief of security and his wife.

"Who's that?" Ellen cooed.

"Professor Philip Boynton, professor of science," Lisa smirked.

"Still boy-crazy, our little Ellen," Raquel sighed with a shake of her head.

"Very much a bookworm. And that's something coming from me," Lisa teased.

"Speaking of books, he could be the leading man in a romance novel," Ellen tittered. She left her friends to wrangle an impromptu chance meeting with the handsome professor.

Tina joined the ladies as if to take the socialite's place within the group. She resumed her serious, aloof attitude. Despite Lisa's and Raquel's light-hearted chatter, she did not join in.

Twirling her flaxen tresses, Ellen approached Boynton conversing with two of his less-appealing colleagues.

"Hello, Professor Boynton," Ellen purred as she pranced up to Boynton.

The security chief was pleased that his wife was pleased that the young socialite found new prey.

"Do we know each other?" he stammered perplexed.

"Not yet, handsome," Ellen wheedled. "I'm Ellen and you're a science professor. You wouldn't specialize in human biology, would you?"

"As a matter of fact, yes, I do," Boynton said surprised at the accuracy of her guess and missing the innuendo completely.

Tina issued a respectful, "Professor" as she walked by.

"Miss Canfield," Boynton acknowledged perfunctorily.

Ellen's next flirtation was stymied.

A bell tinkled to signal the end of the fashionable soiree.

"Excuse me, please," Tina gave a curt dip of the head. "Thank you for a lovely evening and the wonderful opportunity." She disappeared among the gaggle.

The crowd became spectators as they watched Raquel ceremoniously lift up the Fabergé Egg and its stand between her delicate snow-colored hands. Greg carefully hoisted the glass dome. A beefy supercilious security guard hefted the pillar. The three of them formed a regal procession from the far of the hall to the windowless alcove. They advanced slowly.

The nameless security guard placed the pillar in the center of the ten-by-ten room, a rather large secure closet of sorts. He stood to one side. The remaining crowd peered within.

The specially constructed chamber functioned as a combination showroom and small bank vault. Inside was decorated in the epitome of Russian aristocracy, the throne room of the Winter Palace. White round pillars with gold leafing at the top and bottom graced the sides. Neo-classical gold floral designs in white sections hovered overhead. The floor design belonged on an ancient Greek vase. Its rococo motif in shades ranging from gold to brown spread out before the guests. Painted on the far wall featured a replicated scarlet and gold throne framed by a similarly colored curtain adorned with the royal Romanov crest and two elegant pillars on either side. The seven-foot-tall, three-foot wide painted throne dominated.

"St. George's Hall and Apollo Room," Lisa smiled with more than a little sense of awe to no one in particular.

In front of her guests, Raquel reverently placed the Egg on top of the pillar. Greg ceremoniously positioned the crystal dome protection over the Egg.

The guard and Raquel withdrew out of the bay alcove. Greg closed and loudly clicked the door lock as their remaining guests bore witness.

The Cannings began to bid farewell to each of the guests individually as the service staff finished cleaning. They dismissed the security crew. They shut off the lights and secured the library doors before exiting.

"Come on, hot stuff. Let's grab a night cap," Raquel giggled as she led Ellen away from Professor Boynton. On her other arm, she had Gregorio in tow.

Grinning, Lisa politely nodded at Boynton as she passed him. He responded in kind.

At Raquel's request, the trio paused outside the Library in the warm summer evening.

Ellen saw Boynton descend the library stairs. Stepping away from Raquel, she pulled a cigarette from her silver and black case. For effect, she batted her sparkling brown eyes at Boynton. As the science professor fumbled for a match, Lisa countered and produced a lighter. Boynton demurely lowered his head and continued on his way.

Tina giggled as Lisa blocked Ellen's second attempt at Boynton.

Ellen and Lisa waited as Raquel locked the anteroom door and Gregorio set the burglar alarms.

"We want to personally make certain every security measure is set in place for ourselves, security-wise" Gregorio insisted.

"No security guards stationed inside?" Lisa asked.

"Security guards can be too easily bribed, you know," Raquel countered. "Just an additional ounce of prevention."

Spoken like someone who has bribed enough of security guards to lose faith in them, Ellen discerned.

Raquel added with a wink, "Campus security will do just fine. They can keep an eye on each other."

The quartet piled into a luxurious maroon Cadillac—the girls in the back seat and Gregorio driving. They headed north along Sather Road and crossed a couple streets to enjoy a few late night cocktails and cigarettes at the villa of the University President Robert Sproul. Sproul surreptitiously allowed the generous donors to have the run of the house unencumbered while he was away tending his duties as provost of the University of California at Los Angeles.

Raquel and Gregorio casually entered the Mediterranean style-chateau set in the middle of two-and-a-half acres. They led Lisa and Ellen inside.

Because Kai was excused for the evening, Gregorio played the part of a garrulous bartender for the remainder of the night. Alcohol-inspired reminisces and laughter filled in the elegant salon.

The night wrapped up with Ellen and Raquel reluctantly promising to meet Lisa for a little afternoon fencing workout.

Midnight chimes urged everyone to say their good-nights and retreat to their respective lodgings.

Lisa accompanied Ellen on the path back to their old sorority house. They parted company with a remainder of the fencing workout.

The Alpha Phi Beta Sorority House, like the rest of the campus, was closed for all practical purposes during the summer semester. Only a handful of sorority sisters stayed over the summer months and they allowed Ellen free reign with an extra key. Ellen didn't need it. She was quite experienced at sneaking in and out of the sorority house. That night, her skill came in handy after she donned the black cloak, white gown, and gossamer mask of the Domino Lady.

Despite the cloudless celestial sky, the cape's silky ebony obscured the pristine ivory of the satin gown as the Domino Lady slinked out of the two-story stucco house and meandered from shadow to shadow back to the Doe Memorial Library. Along the way, she dodged the sporadic campus security patrol. At the Library, she skillfully disarmed the security alarm system with ease. She adeptly picked each lock which failed to prevent her unauthorized entrance into the darkened library hall.

The ambient moonlight radiated in through high closed windows to illuminate the pathway to the Fabergé Egg through the center of the hall to the security alcove. The high round cocktail tables from the reception were removed. Wooden chairs and polished tables remained against the bookshelves instead of their traditional cafeteria style arrangement. The university janitorial staff wouldn't arrive until late morning. They'd be in no hurry to restore the decor because of the negligible attendance during summer sessions.

The Domino Lady silently charged down the main aisle. Within minutes, she reached the alcove. Its door was open. She suddenly grew suspicious at how unsecure an Imperial curio of such value appeared to be.

As she stepped closer to her prize, the crunch of broken glass indicated the anemic attempt of glass-domed security on top of the pedestal failed. Her eyes accustomed to the dark revealed the wire holder in the center of the pedestal held nothing except a stiff paper card on the tiny throne.

The Domino Lady plucked the dark card from the holder. Without reading it, she backed out of the alcove, hastened to the exit, and slipped the card into her lace leg garter next to a syringe containing knock-out serum. She left the door ajar.

If her suspicion was correct, she needed to delay her egress by locking each door and restoring the burglar alarm system.

This jewel heist went from mundane to peculiar very quickly, she thought.

After the Domino Lady eventually reached the outside burglar alarm, she began re-splicing the wires. She turned and detected a black-clothed figure drifting gracefully toward her.

The physical shadow closed in on her before she could react. With a quick flick of the arm, a hand blow struck the Domino Lady on the side of her head. Stunned, she staggered back. She tried to focus; only to see her attacker's face was wrapped in a dark cowl that only allowed exposed the eyes.

"Hey, what's going on over there?" Two of the U. of C.'s finest rushed the dark figures on the cement landing of the library. Drawing their guns, they shouted warnings not to move. The University allowed the use of side arms temporarily while the Fabergé Egg was on exhibit.

The Domino Lady's assailant shifted attention and leaped over the stairs. Coming down, one foot disarmed the patrolman on the right and the opposite hand disarmed the officer on the left. As the figure landed, the arms and hands blurred as the two security officers stopped and fell down onto the parkway.

Another impressive leap and the dark form returned to the exact spot facing the prepared Domino Lady.

Recovered from the stunning blow, she blocked the next thrust with her arm and countered the expected kick with a halting dropkick of her own.

Silently, the black-garbed fighting machine dropped back and performed a series of straight vertical punches toward her, alternating the right and left arms.

Obviously, the move was designed to intimidate her.

She played along and dropped to a knee.

"Please, don't hurt me," she whimpered in a breathy voice.

The phantom-like assailant slinked in for a numbing strike. The Domino Lady responded with a judo grapple and jabbed the syringe into the nearest leg.

Before the full contents could be injected, the attacker slapped her hand and sent the hypodermic needle flying.

Before the Domino Lady could take her next breath, the black-garbed figure staggered and collapsed at her feet.

The Domino Lady dragged the unconscious form over to the bushes. She located and capped the empty syringe before cramming it back into her leg garter. She finished re-arming the burglar alarm.

The Domino Lady expected a back-up patrol to be arriving soon when no one checked in within the required fifteen-minute interval. She grabbed and lugged her mysterious attacker away from the Library. Pulling the body into the nearest building, she hauled it up the cement stairs and deftly picked yet another door lock. Inside, she located the closest washroom. She flicked on the lights and saw a fire safety hose reel. Pulling the reel, she wrapped up the foiled mugger with the fire hose like Boris Karloff in "The Mummy."

The Domino Lady took stock of the attacker's garb. Besides leather gloves, a thin black jacket, and trousers with light sandals afforded the only body covering.

Grabbing a handful of the hooded cowl, she yanked it off to reveal the face of Kai, the Canning's Chinese servant.

Wetting the cowl with cold water from the faucet, she slapped Kai's face with it to resuscitate him as the effects of the knock-out drug began to wear off. He responded quickly.

"What da hell's goin' on, lady?" groaned Kai. His face reddened with anger as he wiggled to loosen his cotton-fiber constraints.

"Don't bother, chum," the Domino Lady growled deeply.

"Let me outta dis ting," he demanded.

"You sound like you're from the Bronx," she said in a hoarse whisper.

"Yeah, dat's right. Ya gotta a problem wit dat?"

"Your employers have been telling people that you're a mute from China."

"Yeah, well, dat's da racket, I s'pose." Kai stopped struggling. "I'm as Chinese as chop suey."

The Domino Lady knew chop suey, a term roughly translated to "odds and ends" or "leftovers", was a dish invented in New York City about forty years back.

"What're doing sneaking around campus in the middle of the night?" the

...to reveal the face of Kai...

Domino Lady asked. She sensed feminine wiles weren't going to influence a trussed-up man desperate to escape.

"Aww, go soak your head," Kai jeered.

The Domino Lady drew her hand back to slap him, but reconsidered.

"You were going to steal the Fabergé Egg, weren't you?"

Kai's eyes widen but his lips tightened.

"Well, I got news for you. Someone else beat us to it," she said pouting.

"Youse lyin' ta me," he spat back.

"No, in fact, I'd like to call a truce."

"A what?"

"An armistice."

"Youse surrender?"

"No, I want to stop fighting each other. I don't have the Egg and you don't have it."

"How do I know dat yah don't got it?"

"I'd let you search me if I didn't think you'd enjoy it so much," she smirked.

"Hey, I'm engaged, you ditzy broad."

That little bit of revelation meant he no longer considered her the enemy.

The Domino Lady reached under the slit of her gown and retrieved the black calling card she retrieved from the Egg's stand. As she suspected, it read "Compliments of the Domino Lady" in white letters.

"Hey, where'd ya get dat? Ya frisk me when I was knocked out or sumtin'?" Kai shouted indignantly.

"No. I found this in place of the Egg."

Kai knitted his eyebrows and his lips tightened again.

"Let me outta dis ting. I got sumtin to show yah," he said.

The Lady Domino relented but produced her silver-plated .22 automatic pistol as a warning.

A few twists and yanks on the fire hose freed Kai.

He rubbed his gloved wrists and ankles. Staring at the gun aimed at him, he slid his hand inside his jacket and produced a black card with white ink.

"I got da same ting."

The Domino Lady snatched it out of his hand and gasped, "What's going on?"

"Ya said we had an armtwist? Wat's wid da gat?"

"Tell me your story first," she said with a slight wave of the handgun.

Kai shrugged his shoulders and exhaled.

"Dis was gonna be my last job for da Cannins'. Dey treat me like a jerk anyway. I was s'pose to swipe da flibbertigibbet egg. I was s'pose to leave dis card after I pocketed da crummy egg."

"Someone's playing me. I thought the Cannings were wealthy."

"Sure. Dey got plenty of dough. But dey always want more. Greedy, yah know. I was gonna heist the egg and take a powder. Den me and Jasmine. Jasmine, dat's my fiancé. We could live happily ever after. Away from da Cannins'. Jasmine knows all 'bout da Cannins and wants me out."

"You do a lot of work like this for the Cannings?"

"Yeah. A heist here and dere. Da pay is okay. But dey been asking me ta do some more risky stuff. Like dis. I want out, but dey ain't making it easy for me."

"You steal the Egg for them in the first place."

"Nah, I don't know where it came from. One day Cannin' just showed up wid it. Raquel, she was tickled pink. I stoled lots of other stuff, though."

"How do they get it through customs and insured?"

"Dey pay people off, what didja think?"

Corrupt officials was a touchy subject for the Domino Lady every since her father, Owen Patrick, was murdered by a gunman hired by corrupt politicians.

Momentarily distracted by remembrances of her father, she lowered her .22.

Kai noticed it. He jerked out a leg and tripped the Domino Lady to the tile floor. In a fluid motion, he hopped up and bolted out the bathroom door.

The Domino Lady cursed her momentary lapse, but she had both calling cards now. She also knew the only place where Kai was headed.

Slipping outside, she spotted the security back-up helping their comrades. She easily avoided their attention to pursue Kai. She fled across the campus like a cloud's shadow over the earth during a sunny day. Minutes later, she revisited her drinking hole from earlier.

This is getting to be habit-forming, she mused as she intuitively picked yet another lock. This one was attached to the front door of the President's House.

An unlit porch and the stygian foyer hid the Domino Lady's entrance as she crept inside to listen to an escalating argument.

"I tell yah. She had nuttin' to do wid it."

"But the Domino Lady is here? She's supposed to be miles south of here," boomed another male voice, obviously Gregorio.

"White moo-moo. Black mask. Fights like a champ. Just like da papers say."

"If you're lying to me. Turn out your pockets!"

"I ain't got no pockets."

Staying in the shadows, the Domino Lady leaned closer to see Gregorio holding a .45.

"If you're lying to me, Kai, I'll kill you. This complicates matters. I didn't count on the actual Domino Lady stealing the Egg."

"I tol' yah. She didn' have it."

"She's probably lying. How would she know it was here?"

A female voice belonging to Raquel reasoned, "It was in more than a couple of the society pages. That was the point of this, wasn't it? Make it discreetly yet publicly known about the Fabergé Egg. So we could collect the insurance money."

"And still retain possession of the Egg," Gregorio added.

"Such a cliché," whispered the Domino Lady in a hoarse voice as she stuck her .22 out of the foyer. She remained eclipsed in the shadows to avoid providing an easy target for Gregorio. Although her face was shrouded, the shadows merely served to enhance her voluptuous curves.

Both Gregorio and Kai mouth's went dry at the sight of the enticing outline of her side breast and hip.

"It's cliché because it's a proven revenue source," Raquel said as she pointed another .45 automatic toward the foyer.

"Shooting each other will solve nothing," the Domino Lady rasped. "I don't have the Fabergé Egg."

"I tol' yah," Kai added.

"Why should I believe you?" Gregorio countered.

"Why would I be here if I did?"

"To steal from us," Gregorio spat.

"Shhh, Gregorio. Why *are* you here then?" Raquel demanded.

"I want to know why *you* wanted to implicate *me* in the Fabergé Egg theft?"

"Simple. You're a known jewel thief. Obviously, a little too well-known from the look of things. Someone else had the same idea as us," Raquel responded. "But the papers said you used a .45."

"The .45 made my hand look fat, so I switched to the .22 for a more slimming effect," the Domino Lady joked.

"No insurance company would question it if they thought you stole it. The cops'll go through the motions of searching for the Fabergé but they wouldn't find any trace of it. No one would suspect us. We'd get the insurance money and a hefty sum from the University when we sue for their carelessness on whatever grounds our lawyers can dig up," Raquel explained.

Gregorio growled at Raquel. "Why the hell are you telling her all this?"

"It doesn't matter. She's inconsequential, darling," she snapped back.

Relying on the couple's bickering as a diversion, Kai sprung toward the .22, but the Domino Lady withdrew before he could lay a hand on her. The only thing she left in her wake was the wooden slam of the front door.

"Forget her, Kai," Gregorio ordered. "But I don't trust what she says anyway."

"She doesn't matter. Whether or not she has it, the Egg is gone," Raquel discounted.

"True. There's nothing to do until the police contact us tomorrow," Gregorio said as he looked out upon a desolate front lawn and secured the front door again. He double-checked the doorknob's lock.

With only about an hour left before daybreak, the Domino Lady snuck back into the sorority house undetected. Stripping down to her gauzy bra and panties, she stashed her costume and gear away. She crawled into bed.

Ellen rubbed the side of her head. She conceded Kai's keen fighting skill was admirable. Thoughts of hiring him away from the Cannings to teach her a few tricks lulled her to sleep.

Ellen didn't wake up until shortly after 10 a.m. The extra sleep helped her recuperate after her late night excursion and from the encounter with the nimble Kai. Others viewed it as merely part of her spoiled dilettante lifestyle.

Ellen devoured a modest repast of toast and coffee but skipped her late morning cigarette. She donned a pair of white tennis shorts, matching top, and sneakers to meet her friends at the women's gym on the university's south end – the impressive Phoebe Apperson Hearst Memorial Gymnasium

As Ellen crossed the campus, she beheld the expected commotion at the Library. She considered playing the part of a self-absorbed ingénue and wandered toward the flashing lights. As she scrutinized the curious gawkers, a beanstalk of a biology professor aroused her interest once again.

"Hello, Philip," Ellen purred as her slender fingers caressed his broad shoulder. "What's the brouhaha, handsome?"

Before Boynton could answer, a strained feminine voice screamed, "My Fabergé Egg! It has been stolen!"

Framed by the library doors, Raquel dramatically struck an overdramatic pose with her arms splayed only to faint into her husband's waiting arms.

Navy-blue uniformed police weaved among turquoise uniforms of the campus security. The Berkeley Police gathered to render aid to the devastated couple.

Campus security retreated sheepishly. The only element missing from this dramatic tableau were reporters from the local newspapers.

"Typical Raquel. You can fill me in as you escort me to the Hearst gymnasium, handsome," Ellen coaxed Boynton away from the scene of the crime.

"I can direct you if you don't know the way," Boynton offered. His academic curiosity aroused by the melodrama unfolding before him.

"Please, Philip. I have to meet Lisa there. With all this rampant crime, I need a strong man to protect me," Ellen batted her engaging cinnamon eyes at the hapless science professor with the sparkling blue eyes.

Male protective instinct fell prey to the rose petal-like lips and the partially exposed valley of tan lines between Ellen's V-necked tennis top.

Arm-in-arm, they strolled south to the women's gymnasium. Boynton informed a breathless Ellen how a janitor alerted authorities after discovering the unlocked door and the stolen artifact. Coming to the gymnasium, he described the arrival of police, campus security, and the Cannings. Chivalrously, he opened the door for Ellen. They lingered in the gym's corridor area.

As Boynton finished telling her as much as he knew, Ellen inquired, "Dinner tonight?"

Somewhat dazed by her abruptness, Boynton beamed and nodded.

"Call me later?"

A peck on his cheek and she disappeared up the stairs into one of the inner gymnasiums. Boynton meandered back to the Library and its ongoing mystery.

Lisa grinned as she saw her friend strut through the gym doors.

"You beat Raquel here. She's probably had some emergency like a broken nail. You'll find a spare fencing uniform in the locker room," Lisa instructed as she stretched and warmed up for the exercise.

"Raquel won't be coming," Ellen lamented."It seems her Fabergé Egg had gotten itself stolen." She weaved her way around the gymnast equipment to the area set up for fencing.

"You're joking," Lisa stopped.

Ellen repeated Boynton's account of the morning's activities.

"We should go and check on her," Lisa said.

"Hold on, my dear. No use us getting in the way. There's nothing we can do for her at the moment. She'll be preoccupied with the police and reporters for quite a while. We'll check on her later. A little fencing came kill some time."

At first, Lisa was taken aback by Ellen's seemingly insensitive sentiment, but she reluctantly agreed that there was a certain logic to it. She realized the police investigation would require Gregorio and Raquel's full, undivided cooperation with statements and paperwork. Admittedly, Lisa and Ellen would only be in the way. She had to admit, Raquel would take her time to play it up for the newspapers. Fencing could provide a brief diversion rather than uselessly fretting about Raquel, callous as it seemed.

Ellen found the padded jacket with chest protector, breeches, gloves, plastron for her arm, and steel mesh mask laid out for her.

"This chest protector is rather confining, isn't it?" Ellen complained as she exited the locker room.

"It's required covering for women fencers. Most women fencers are not as developed as you," Lisa chuckled.

"Foil or epee?" Ellen asked.

"Foil. It's lighter for your delicate arms," Lisa mocked.

The spark of friendly competition flared in Ellen's eyes as she spread her shapely legs and reached for her toes.

After the stretching exercises, they assumed the traditional fencing pose as they faced each other. They pointed their front foot at their opponent, with their back foot perpendicular.

Lisa emphasized, "A reminder—the torso is the only target area. Arms, legs, and head are off-limits."

"Back and groin okay?" Ellen as she slipped the mask over her face.

"Yep. This' going to be fun. En garde!" Lisa smirked and lunged. She nailed Ellen in the right shoulder.

"Point for me," Lisa said. Ellen replied with a riposte. Lisa parried and the match had commenced. The foils swished side to side, up and down. Lunges were dodged and blocked. Thrusts ranged high outside to low inside and low outside to high inside. Ellen spun and Lisa waltzed. Minutes passed quickly as the fencers capered gracefully back and forth, never leaving the rubber piste strip.

Naturally, Lisa maintained the upper hand, but Ellen never dropped her guard or weakened her position. That's why they enjoyed fencing each other so much. They briefly forgot about Raquel and focused on each other.

Lisa countered Ellen's lunge and attacked the left shoulder but Ellen parried. The gym door banged open and diverted Lisa's attention. Ellen scored a direct hit on Lisa's right shoulder.

Before Ellen could brag, Tina's voice erupted from the doorway.

"Professor Brown! Professor Brown?" she screamed desperately looking around, awaiting for a response. She was still wearing the dark green dress, but it was severely rumpled.

Lisa lifted her fencing mask. "Over here. What's the matter?"

"I didn't know who else to go to. Professor Boynton said you were here. I've been up all night," she gasped. "The Egg. It's a forgery, a counterfeit."

The silence was deafening as Tina dropped the bombshell. She meandered around the parallel bars, pommel horse, and horizontal bars scattered throughout the gymnasium.

Ellen and Lisa and Tina shifted stares from one to another and then back.

Ellen grappled with the fact that a simple theft of a Fabergé Egg was wildly spinning out of control. She had no idea how out of control it was about to become.

Tina then opened her hand and the "stolen" Fabergé Egg glimmered in it.

"How did it come into your possession?" demanded Lisa, tossing the foil aside.

An amateur beat two experienced jewel thieves to the punch, Ellen mused.

"I compared it with my notes. They don't match. It's a counterfeit, a fake," Tina erupted.

"But it's insured. Its authenticity was verified by an expert," Lisa balked.

Not if that someone was paid off, Ellen thought.

"It's not the authentic Alexander III Commemorative Fabergé Egg. It's bogus." Tina emphasized indignantly.

"Tina! I don't care why you have it!" Lisa hollered with restraint.

"How did you get it?" Ellen interrupted in an effort to give Lisa a moment to compose herself.

"I ducked into a small storage room when everyone was leaving. The throne was painted over the door, disguising it. After the Library closed, I snuck out and took the Egg. Then I hid back in the storage closet until this morning. When the janitor left to notify campus security, I was able to sneak out. I blended in with the onlookers during the resulting commotion. I went back to my apartment and retrieved my notes. Now the Library is crowded again with police," Tina blurted out.

Spilling out sheets of papers from a manila folder, Tina lectured, "Long story short. Currently, six of the fifty-two Fabergé Eggs are unaccounted for. The Imperial Eggs of the Romanovs, the Russian aristocracy. The Cannings claimed a "lost" Egg just happened to come into their possession mysteriously. But they must've had it fabricated. Here's the only known photograph of the Alexander III Commemorative Egg. The forgery was obviously made from a copy of this photograph. But not a perfect copy."

She laid out handwritten notes on the pommel horse. She plucked out a black-and-white photograph.

The image featured an egg with three sections of minute leafy borders. Only one side of the Egg was visible. The top showed a trapezoid and two halves of wreaths and laurels encircling a star. The mid-section suggested four squares but only the front clearly displayed designed clusters of diamond-set baskets, flowers, and ribbons. Four upside-down hearts acting as the pedestal holder hid the base.

"It certainly looks the same as Raquel and Gregorio have...er *had*," Ellen said.

"Yes. That's why I had to consult my notes. But the details on the base are all wrong."

"The diamonds and gold could be phony as well," Lisa hypothesized.

That's why they needed Kai to steal it last night. So the forgery wouldn't be discovered when the University studied it, Ellen deduced.

At this point, Lisa naturally took charge.

"We need to tell Raquel as soon as possible. We can't delay. She needs to know now," Lisa instructed.

"She may still be at the Library with the police or talking to reporters," Ellen said.

"Or with the university staff. Ellen, you and I will get changed. Tina, come with us," Lisa directed.

Tina's head bobbed up and down like a rubber ball and followed the women into the locker room.

Ellen snatched the Fabergé Egg from Tina. She gently deposited it inside Lisa's locker and covered it with the fencing mask.

"Lock it in here. It wouldn't do to have you wandering around campus with stolen property," Ellen suggested with a wink.

"Sounds like a plan," Lisa nodded.

"You talk to Raquel. I've made plans with Philip. We've a dinner date. He seemed friendly with the chief of security," Ellen pattered as she peeled off the constraining fencing uniform.

As Lisa slid out of her jacket and breeches, she shook her head at Ellen.

"You knew what's going on and arranged a date in the middle of it?" she scolded. "You are so inconsiderate. To think I let you convince me to ignore Raquel and fence. We've got important matters to attend to."

Ellen stood in tight lacy bra and panties caressing her luscious breasts and thighs. With her hands on her curvaceous hips in annoyance, she faced Lisa. This wasn't the first time she received a lecture from Lisa.

"Do we have to do *this* again, Lisa?"

"Seriously, Ellen. Why do you do that? You're an educated woman. Why do you insist on playing the coquette? Take this situation seriously instead of playing the vamp," Lisa chided.

"Seriously, Lisa. I like men and, well, basically, it's fun. Since my father died," her voice cracked a bit. "It's fun, pure and simple. That's all there is to it."

Once again, Ellen Patrick was reminded of how her father was murdered in

"You knew what's going on..."

cold blood during a crime orchestrated by corrupt government officials.

Lisa shrugged her shoulders. She knew her friend was more complicated than she led on. Annoying as she found it, she'd always allowed her dear friend some leeway.

Tina sat on the bench and stared off to the side.

Ellen and Lisa dressed in awkward silence.

In an effort to ease the tension, Ellen said, "In the words of our dear Dorothy Parker, 'Men seldom make passes at girls who wear glasses'."

"And those men are asses," Lisa shot back.

The old friends let out a much-needed therapeutic chuckle. Tina smiled in relief.

The three women swept out of the women's gymnasium and trotted down the stairs.

Over at the crime scene, the Berkeley police scampered in and out of the Library. The campus security milled around outside the grounds trying to corral newspaper reporters. The Cannings languished with annoyed countenances as university administrators attempted to placate the millionaire couple.

"How'd you get past the police?" Ellen asked Tina.

"It's campus security, Ellen. Not exactly a league of Dick Tracies," she said sardonically. "I just walked by them as they scrambled around trying to figure out what to do."

As she lit up a cigarette, Ellen gleaned the gawkers and located Boynton. She exhaled a lazy plume. She tossed a smoky wave in his direction. He blushed.

Lisa smacked the saucy romantic on her shoulder. "Raquel," she gestured frantically with her other hand. It was frantic but not futile.

Recognition flashed in Raquel's sharp eyes and then relief. She excused herself and minced over to Ellen and Lisa.

"I don't have time to chit-chat, girls. As much as I'd like to relive old times, you can see I'm in the middle of a rather serious situation right now," Raquel hissed in gritted teeth.

"The Fabergé Egg. Tina says it's counterfeit. And, ahem, she has proof," Lisa whispered conveniently omitting the part of Tina being in possession of the Egg.

Raquel's eyes flared at Tina.

Tina's focus shifted to her feet.

Ellen rocked back and forth to give her friends the impression that her interests lay elsewhere. The Domino Lady was formulating a plan while Ellen overtly flirted with a dashing albeit callow academic.

"Ellen is otherwise engaged, but we need to get together. Please don't tell the police yet," Lisa pleaded.

"She has a date with that egghead?" Raquel smirked. "You can do so much better, honey. Hook yourself a well-to-do husband."

Ellen scowled at Raquel.

Raquel sighed, "Fine. Gregorio and I need to finish with the police and the reporters. We still have to contact our attorneys and insurance company."

Ellen interjected, "Why don't you meet at the President's House later tonight? You can sort it out privately. Take your time."

"Fine! Don't mention its authenticity to anyone until we see this so-called evidence," Raquel insisted.

Lisa and Tina agreed.

Raquel stormed off in a huff.

"This doesn't concern me, does it?"

"Raquel's your friend."

"And she'll have her silly Egg back. Tina will provide proof that it's a fake, Lisa. Everything will work itself. Maybe Philip may have learned something from the Chief. We'll catch up tomorrow. I promise."

Ellen allowed a sly wink at her potential paramour who was at that moment chatting with a very red-face security chief.

"This is honestly out of my depth and you know it, Lisa" admitted the golden-haired socialite. "I feel for Raquel. But I'm more invested in my rendezvous with Philip." She crushed out her cigarette.

Lisa reluctantly agreed. Ellen had no reason to accompany them to the President's House. She also wished to avoid further awkwardness.

Ellen jogged off to join up with Boynton. As she slid her arm into his, the chief of security tipped his cap to her. Then he politely excused himself from the young couple.

Lisa and Tina returned to the gymnasium to collect the notes and prepare for their conversation with Gregorio and Raquel.

As the excitement at the Library died down, Ellen and Philip's date commenced. It proceeded as expected. A leisurely walk around campus, an early dinner, and a cocktail were all the romance they had time to share. Since Boynton had an early morning department conference, Ellen didn't need to concoct a reason to end the date.

The college professor dropped off the fetching socialite at the sorority house as the sun drooped lower onto the horizon. A twilight kiss completed the tender affair. He dreamily drove off into the setting sun.

Before twilight gave way to dusk, a white gown squeezed Ellen's curves and a black cape hugged her kissable shoulders. A sable domino mask graced her Nordic features transforming her once again to the daring young adventuress.

As the night covered the sky, the Domino Lady glided across the campus amid the eerie shades cast by a full moon in another cloudless sky.

In minutes, she arrived at the gymnasium for women to collect her prize. She manipulated her friends to meet at the President's House so the Fabergé Egg would be unguarded in Lisa's locker.

Easy pickings, she thought.

Suddenly, it was too easy.

The front door to the building was ajar, just like the alcove door was the night before.

Using her pencil flashlight, the Domino Lady entered and coasted through the corridors past darkened offices and locker rooms to the stairs. She ascended the steps and detected harsh voices arguing. To complicate matters, the bitter quarrel reverberated inside the specific gymnasium connected to the specific locker room that concealed the Fabergé Egg under a woman's fencing mask.

Not surprisingly, the door to the gymnasium was unbolted.

The Domino Lady silently eased the door open. Even her jaded eyes were astonished at the sight.

Gregorio and Raquel each held their respective .45 automatics. One on Lisa and the other on Tina. Kai, dressed as their valet, stood by his employers' sides.

"Where is it?" Gregorio demanded.

"Put the gun away!" Lisa shot back.

"Answer my husband," Raquel shouted.

"But it's a fake," Tina reiterated.

"You fool. We need the Egg. We don't need you. One last time! Where did you hide the Egg in here?" Gregorio said as he aimed at Tina.

"Yah said no one was gonna get hurt, boss" Kai growled as he stepped between Gregorio and Tina.

"You realize we're in a secluded area. No one will hear a gunshot!" Gregorio threatened.

"Dat's if yah gets a chance," Kai warned as he threw a punch.

Gregorio pulled the trigger twice and Kai fell down with two bloody holes in his chest. Raquel did not react but continued to focus on Lisa with her automatic.

A weak groan rose from Kai's body as it twitched.

Raquel turned and fired a final shot into Kai's head The callous execution served to further intimidate the two unarmed women.

"I've had enough of his impertinence. He had the audacity to forget his place. Be it as it may, now you know we mean business, tell me," Gregorio spit the words out between his gritted teeth.

"It's in the locker room," Tina whispered as she backed away from the pools of crimson circulating at her feet.

"Good girl," Raquel said as the corners of her mouth curled up. She poised her gun toward the dark-haired collegiate.

"That's my cue!" The Domino Lady yelled from the doorway.

"Damn you. I knew you were involved," Gregorio bellowed as he fired two shots at the curvaceous figure in white prancing across the gymnasium floor between a pommel horse and parallel bars.

Raquel also fired toward the approaching black-caped dynamo.

Lisa tackled Tina to a floor mat to protect her protégé from the wild gun shots.

The Domino Lady's cape took a lead slug meant for her as she closed in on the murderous millionaires. She leapt up and seized the hanging still rings. With the grace of an Olympian, she circumnavigated the rounds from each of the automatics. She twirled through the air. Angling her body, she collided on top of Gregorio. Her mere one-hundred-and-twenty pounds were enough to disarm him and render him unconscious.

Once Raquel knew her husband was no longer in her line of fire, she aimed at the back of the Domino Lady. As she squeezed the trigger, she felt a sharp prick in her shoulder. Her shot went wild into the wooden floor.

Eyes blazing, she turned to the source. Lisa wielded a foil and prepared to strike again. Her foot directed toward Raquel.

"En garde!" Lisa enunciated with precision.

The foil's tip glistened with red. The rubber cap removed. The blood was common red, not royal blue like Raquel claimed. That may have infuriated Raquel more than not killing the Domino Lady.

With homicide burning in her eyes, Raquel once again shifted the automatic toward her former friend. Greed was her only ally now.

Before Raquel could pull the trigger, Lisa lunged and slid the blood-christened tip of the foil deep inside the gun barrel. Only one with Lisa's expert sword skill could have deftly maneuvered such a feat.

"If you pull that trigger, the blast will backfire. It will definitely ruin your lovely manicure and most likely damage your dainty hand. In all probability, even permanently scar your flawless face," Lisa snarled.

Stunned by the possibility of personal injury, Raquel visibly loosened her grip and Lisa flicked the gun out of her hand with a twist of the sword. Zorro would have been envious.

The Domino Lady let the automatic topple at her feet. She kicked it away and it skidded toward Kai's corpse. She pointed a silver-plated .22 at Lisa.

"Now, put down the sword," the Lady Domino growled in a hoarse whisper.

Lisa let the foil clatter to the floor. Raquel, she could bluff, but the Domino Lady was an unknown factor.

Hiking up her gown, the Domino Lady withdrew a re-filled hypodermic needle from the garter around a sylphlike thigh. She stepped toward Raquel.

"Please, mercy," Raquel whimpered.

"You offered your valet no mercy," the Domino Lady sneered. The Domino Lady menacingly drew closer to Raquel to render her unconscious.

"He, he was only a servant. A Chinese one at that," Raquel derided. She jerked to avoid the Domino Lady's injection. She spotted her .45 lying on the floor just on the other side of Kai's body. She dashed toward the gun. In her rush, she slipped on Kai's slick blood. Her feet flew up in the air as if they were kicked out from underneath her. Her neck cracked as it hit the floor before the rest of her body followed. Her head tilted at an unnatural angle.

Kai's final strike from beyond the grave, the Domino Lady thought.

Lisa hastened to Raquel's body. She leaned over and let out a soft sob. "She's dead."

The Domino Lady plunged the needle into Lisa's neck. She injected only half its contents into her friend. She caught the history professor before she collapsed. She laid her gently on a nearby mat.

"Now, you!" the Domino Lady barked.

"It's just us now, Ellen," Tina said smartly. "You can drop the malevolent accent."

The Domino Lady cackled softly. "I don't know what you mean."

"Raquel and Lisa could never imagine their boy-crazed classmate would be capable of being the Domino Lady. I'm not hampered by any such preconceived notion. Perhaps if it weren't for the gunfire and life-threatening situation, Lisa may have concluded the same. The men you oppose may not notice your hairstyle and make-up, but that, of course, is something a woman always takes note of," Tina explained assuming an air of superiority again.

The Domino Lady plucked off her mask and smirked.

"Thank you for that observation. I'll be sure to remedy that in the future. But I can unmask you as well."

"I have nothing to hide," Tina declared.

Even without the mask, the Domino Lady stared down Tina.

"You acted as if the theft of the Fabergé Egg was an impulse. Something that you did rashly after examining it that night at the reception."

"Of course," Tina sputtered.

"Except you left my calling card. That indicates the theft was premeditated. You brought the fake card with you to the reception. Only the Cannings, Kai, and I knew that a Domino Lady calling card was left in place of the Egg. I removed it when I went in to steal the Egg."

Tina acquiesced with a slight shrug of the shoulders. "I wondered what happened to it. I thought campus security simply overlooked it. Or lost it. Or it somehow blew away. I was going to return the Egg with a note stating it was a counterfeit with another Domino Lady calling card," Tina sighed.

"It's obvious you planned on stealing the fake long before attending the reception. You purposely had the closet installed when the alcove was built. You then had the throne painted over its door."

"When I first learned about the Fabergé Egg being loaned to the university, I offered to design the security alcove. But that proves nothing."

"But you did steal it. Why? Why not just reveal it as a fake?"

"Because the University and the Cannings would have covered it up. If the police were involved, then it would become a matter of public record."

"One final observation: The only way you could've definitely have known it was a fake before seeing it was if you were in possession of the genuine Alexander III Commemorative Imperial Easter Egg," Ellen stated with confidence. Tina shrugged nonchalantly.

Ellen made her final pronouncement. "Meaning, naturally, that you must be a member of the Romanov family."

"A weak assumption," Tina sneered.

"Would you deny it? Deny your noble heritage to me?"

Tina's gray-blue eyes sparkled. "I knew we were going to be friends."

They embraced each other.

"Yes, we are. Promise to keep each other's secrets?" the Domino Lady asked as she replaced her mask.

"That's what friends do. And a Romanov is always true to her word," Tina winked as they clasped hands.

"I've a plan that'll leave you in the clear," the Domino Lady said. "But first."

She injected the remaining knock-out drug into Gregorio's neck. Then she detailed her scheme to Tina.

Thirty minutes later, the Domino Lady skulked around the perimeter of the empty President's House. She circled the house twice letting her cape flap unrestrained. It snapped loudly like a whip. She paraded up the front steps and stood on the porch with her hands on her hips. She defiantly appraised the moonlit grounds for any sign of movement. Bracing herself, she kicked in the door. The wooden door jamb cracked. Another kick splintered the doorjamb off the wall. The solid door banged against the wall. As a natural reaction to the force, the door bounced back and slammed shut.

The Domino Lady laughed out loud at the door's ridiculouslessness as an impotent setback to prevent her entrance.

A quick shove and the door swung open. The busted door jamb jammed underneath to keep clear the door, now reduced to a mere piece of lumber.

The Domino Lady thumped her way inside. She proceeded from room to room turning on every lamp and chandelier of every chamber she entered. Light after light glowed like beacons in the darkness outside tracking the Domino Lady's path window by window.

She searched each room for hidden stashes of cash by tossing papers and dumping drawers. As she expected, the foyer, salon, hallways, offices, dining room, and kitchen hid nothing.

Tina's notes lay exposed on the dining room table, but nothing to steal.

The Domino Lady's cape made it appear as if she was floating up the stairs.

The second floor sequestered the bedrooms. That proved to be the location of the Cannings' valuables. The first room was locked. Another swift kick removed the wooden barrier with a sharp bang.

A flip of a light switch revealed Gregorio's open suitcase lay on the bed. Inside were folded clothes but no money belt. She removed any trinkets of any value. The Domino Lady scooped up the cufflinks, pinky ring, and watches on the nearby dresser. She felt like a pirate pillaging a prized conquest.

She dumped the drawers from the dressers. Contents spilled onto the rugs. Shiny baubles glinted in the glow of the overhead chandelier.

Pausing, she considered an array of Raquel's personal effects.

Taking a deep breath, she rifled through Raquel's purses and packed suitcases. She removed all the jewelry and any cash she could find. Kai's blood ended her friend's need to adorn herself in sophisticated elegance, the Domino Lady rationalized. Exquisite and flawless earrings, bracelets, rings, and necklaces filled a handy pillow case from Raquel's side of the bed.

Now she felt like a bit like a ghoul.

After collecting the loot, she lugged the jingling pillow case to the next bedroom.

This door wasn't locked.

The Domino Lady flipped up the toggle light switch. She observed that this room was used by Kai by the servant's garb hanging in the closet. His suitcase lay open on the bed. She plunked the pillow case of loot beside it. She lumbered over to the window and brushed aside the lace curtain. A whiff of stodginess invaded her nostril.

She thought she heard a crumble of gravel and she was correct.

A Buick Cruiser coasted to a stop and hooted its horn. Two campus security guards bounced out of the car.

It's about time, she thought.

As the two security guards rushed through the shattered door with side arms drawn, the Domino Lady slid open the window letting the lace curtains dance as the balmy night air wheezed inside. The guards performed a quick reconnaissance of the first floor then clamored up the stairs to the bedrooms.

The Domino Lady ducked out the window, held onto the window sill, and twisted. She dropped a few feet to the ground and ran post haste to the security squad car.

The keys jangled in the ignition as she plopped down in the driver seat.

It was still running so she released the brake. Hopping out the door, she watched as it slowly taxied down the street away from the President's House.

"Halt," shouted the campus security guard from the open bedroom window.

The Domino Lady waved and flipped her black cape around her white dress. She seemed to vanish from site. Her laughter could be heard leading south to the campus carried along by the summer breeze.

Before exiting the President's House, one of the guards telephoned for back-up from campus security headquarters. Two more cars were dispatched to that location after the security chief severely berated the officer for the loss of a squad car.

Outside the President's House, the other security officer was pre-occupied, chasing the squad car rolling down the driveway onto the lawn into a thicket of trees.

Within minutes, the support arrived with sirens bleating like bulls in their death throes.

The first two guards were scratching their heads pondering how to extricate their ride from a tangle of bushes and tree trunks. They left the scene of the crash to confer with their associates.

"It was the Domino Lady!" said one of the first officers to arrive at the

President's House to shift the focus from the automotive-shrubbery mishmash.

"Are you sure?"

"Well, pretty sure."

"Shouldn't we notify the official police?"

"The chief said not to. At least, not yet. Until we confirm it is the Domino Lady."

"Yeah, he's pissed that we already looking pretty dumb with the whole Egg thing today."

"Not to mention the car!"

More than a hundred yards away, the Domino Lady flung away her ebony cape away from her ivory-covered form like a cloud revealing the moon.

"Hey, boys," she crooned with a hint of a twang. "Looking for little 'ol me?"

She was annoyed she had to wait this long to get their attention.

A hasty wave beckoned and she scampered off toward the north branch of Strawberry Creek. She inhaled the eucalyptus that wafted lightly from the evergreen groves along the creek.

The six campus security guards scrambled like the Keystone Kops to the waiting Buicks.

"Where do you think you two are going?" blurted out one of the drivers with an outstretched arm.

"Wha-wha?" stammered the driver of the tree-impounded squad car.

"You two chase her on foot," came the reply with a grin.

Four security officers slipped inside the cars and saluted their vehicle-challenged compatriots. They sped off away from the steel and granite house south to the eastbound roadway.

The two other officers charged in pursuit of the young adventuress over the university president's grounds toward Strawberry Creek.

The creek was low due to the dry summer season. She could have leapt over but she didn't want to chance slipping into the water.

The Domino Lady carried her onyx-colored stilettos as she raced over the nearest bridge. Her nylon-covered feet offered no sound for the security officers to follow.

They leaped and jumped over roots and between the trees. Reaching a clearing, they spied her at the other end of the bridge.

The Domino Lady performed a pirouette like a woodland nymph. She scooted onto the grass beside a gravel pathway to protect her nyloned feet. She headed south over a roadway with two sets of headlights heading her way. A siren howled at her silhouette. She hurdled over a marble balustrade fence which blocked the squad cars from pursuit.

The landscaping of Haviland Hall afforded her the opportunity to play hide-

and-seek with her uniformed pursuers. She zipped from tree to shrub to bush to tree. The three-story white brick building created additional shades and shadows to confuse her hunters. Only the marbled Pegasuses sculpted in the ornamentation above could track the jewel thief's seemingly erratic movements.

The squad cars with bright headlights dazzling circled Haviland Hall. The cars paused to let two security guards out of the passenger side. They joined the two officers on foot in spreading out to entrap their daring young prey.

Silently, she snuck behind one squad car and skipped over another road to California Hall.

Built in 1905, the authoritative two-story California Hall housed the university's central administration. Stately oak window casing allowed the Domino Lady to stand on the sill and call out to her trackers. Her lithe form was lost among the building's Classical Revival style.

Each security guard uttered a different curse as she drew their attention away from Haviland Hall.

As they closed in, the Domino Lady stepped off the window sill into the evergreen bushes below.

By the time, the two squad cars and four patrolmen arrived at California Hall; she crossed east to the Doe Library.

She led them past the Library. One squad followed on the side road in front and the other pursued on the auxiliary road behind the Library. The others jogged along the checkered-lit grounds on either side to trap her like a scared rabbit into a snare. However, scared was never a word to accurately describe the Domino Lady.

When they reached the other side of the Library, she vanished once again.

Like the aforementioned pursued rabbit, the Domino Lady avoided her hounds by ducking through nearby six-foot bushes. The meticulously trimmed shrubbery surrounded the oldest building on campus, South Hall.

She shot up the wooden porch of the red brick building to wait for her confused uniformed hounds.

She enjoyed this brief respite to catch her breath. She glanced up at the stone bear on the balcony railing above the entrance. She thought she detected the slightest grin on the ursine stonework as if it knew what she had planned.

This was the final leg of her campaign.

Gasping for breath, the four harried security guards appeared at each corner of the four-story building. One squad car rumbled at the north end as its counterpart grumbled on the south roadway.

The two guards on the west side signaled the ones on the east side to join them.

"Hello, boys," she crowed. Her cheeky wink was lost in the dim moon light.

Domino Lady stepped off the window sill ...

They rushed her.

She enveloped herself with her long, flowing cape and vaulted off the porch railing.

The cars turned to shine their headlights to reveal their prey.

Her nimble speed evaded any detection once again.

The drivers even abandoned their cars to locate any trace of the fugitive.

Lacking any professional police training, none of them uncovered any clue of her whereabouts.

Standing near the south branch of Strawberry Creek, the Domino Lady gloated.

Shaking her head at their ineptitude, she yodeled and spread her dark cape wide.

The hunter moon illuminated and accentuated the smoky whiteness of her sublime feminine form. The evening gown deliciously glowed in the reflected light. Long, blonde locks shimmered over her shoulders.

The security officers responded like barracudas attracted to a shiny, silver mackerel. They all forsook the running autos to capture that teasing flirt with their bare hands.

In a hush, the Domino Lady glided over the creek's bridge, past the silent running track, under empty wooden bleachers to her imposing concrete destination, the Hearst Memorial Gymnasium. She faltered on the portico and rested. She pounded on the door as a signal.

Snorting, puffing, and panting, six campus security guards arrived shortly after her. She waited in the shadow of the imposing urn with its leonine gargoyles hovering several feet over her honey blonde tresses. The concrete was still warm from the day's sun. She could feel the heat against her arm. She swore she could smell the cherry blossoms from the trees several yards west of the gymnasium.

The guards drew their side arms on her. Two held flashlights as well. Their light blue uniform shirts darkened with sweat.

The Domino Lady stepped out of the oversized urn's shadow toward the tense security officers. Her hands remained behind her back under her cape. Her ruby red lips glistened against the moonlight.

"Get your hands up!" demanded the youngest campus security guard who was breathing regularly.

The Domino Lady slowly raised her left hand over her head.

"Show us your other hand, missy," ordered another guard in a high pitched tone.

A devious smile widened under her sleek domino mask.

"Is this what you're looking for?" she peeped in feigned innocence.

The Domino Lady lazily swung out her right arm like a broken gate in the soft breeze. She opened her hand and unfurled her slender fingers one by one. The Fabergé Egg's golden trim reflected in the security guards' flashlights.

"Don't come any closer!" spoke her red-rouged lips no longer grinning.

"Is that what I think it is?" gulped a nervous, young guard shaking his pistol as he spoke.

"What do you think it is?"

"The freaking Egg. Is it the Egg?" said a burly dark-haired guard gritting his teeth.

"Of course, it is, silly," the Domino Lady giggled. She sensed the tension rising among the officers. The theft of the Egg was a source of embarrassment for the entire security staff. The merry chase she just led them on added to their frustration. Mocking them wasn't lightening their mood any.

"Put your guns down. They're scaring poor little me," she said with a slight pout.

The youngest officer began to lower his weapon.

"Don't fall for it, Harvey! Police said she's pretty shifty."

The young security guard raised his revolver.

The Domino Lady lowered her left hand in front of her. Her palm inclined as if it could somehow shield herself from one of their bullets.

"Fine. I'll give you this if you let me go," she offered. The Fabergé Egg quivered in her narrow hand.

"That's not going to happen, lady," said the burly officer.

"Hand it over, nice and easy," Harvey said regaining his professional focus.

She took a deep breath letting her breasts protrude against the white bodice of her gown.

"Here you go," she yelled as she lobbed the Egg high into the air. Then she flung her velvety cloak at the armed men.

Startled by the aggressive flap, five pulled their triggers in response. One or two shots banged from each service pistol as the sounds echoed making it sound as if twice as many were fired. The flashes from the muzzles flared like a dazzling strobe light.

Officer Harvey did not shoot. Instead, he dropped his gun and instinctively lunged for the four-inch Fabergé Egg before it could smash to pieces on the cement deck. He ducked under the ensuing gunfire. He was able to snag it in the cradle of his hand preventing the slightest damage to the precious antique.

As the thundering of the shots died down, a blood-wrenching scream resounded within the Hearst building's corridors.

The five guards shifted their aim as the oaken doors burst open.

"Help," wailed Tina. "Help! Please. I think there's a dead man in here."

Confused, the campus security officers looked at one another and then at the rumpled black cape.

"And a, a woman has been injured. Please, help," Tina cried.

Officer Harvey sat up clasping the Fabergé Egg close to his chest. He nodded to assure his comrades that he was unhurt.

"Please, you need to do something," Tina insisted in a desperate voice.

"Check it out," the burly officer directed with a jerk of his revolver.

Three officers followed Tina inside.

Tina led the charge. The footsteps of the four reverberated as they raced down the hall and up the stairs.

Tina leaned into the smaller gymnasium's door to allow the security guard access. She stepped aside as the officers stumbled inside.

They were not prepared for the site of blood and bodies.

"We need to call the police," one of the security guards uttered.

"Yeah," gulped another.

The third simply nodded in agreement.

Within minutes, Berkeley police assumed command of the crime scene with the full consent of campus security. Amid a swarm of professional police activity, the campus security officers and their chief stood docile and timorous to the side near the entrance. Unlike his security staff, the chief's shirt was not sweat stained. Like them, he remained silent.

Police officers stood guard at various stations around the small gym. Detectives examined various sections and gym equipment. Technicians photographed and collected evidence around the bodies of Kai and Raquel. They expertly avoided coagulating blood puddles.

The slight vapor of stagnant body fluids and molding flesh were barely discernible from the natural gymnasium odors of sweat, chalk powder, and old socks with a touch of cordite.

Whether it was the staccato cacophony of the crime scene or the stunning, pungent smelling salts that cause Lisa's eyes to flip open like a pair of car hoods did not matter.

Lisa knew she was in the middle of police activity.

"Lieutenant, over here. She's awake," shouted a police officer in a dark blue uniform.

The college professor straightened up by herself. She was sitting in a wooden folding chair. She focused on the nearby pommel horse to clear her head.

A man in a loose beige suit and chestnut fedora stepped between Lisa and the pommel horse.

The police officer nodded and walked away.

"I'm fine," argued Lisa anticipating the question.

"We need to hear what happened here, Miss Brown," said the sandy-haired police lieutenant in charge.

"Professor Brown. She's a university professor," Tina cut him off as she appeared from behind.

"We have your statement, Miss Canfield. Thank you. Please do not interrupt again," grunted the lieutenant. "Patrolman, please escort Miss Canfield out of here." He pointed near campus security. She did not resist.

When Tina was outside the small gymnasium, the Lieutenant returned his focus to Lisa.

"Now, Professor Brown, what happened?"

"Where's Gregorio, Officer?" Lisa said focusing on her surroundings. The pommel horse and horizontal bars adjusted from fuzzy shapes to defined objects.

"It's Lieutenant. Lieutenant Brown, as a matter of fact," he smiled. "What occurred here tonight?"

"I don't know what Tina told you," Lisa said.

"We need to hear your side of things."

"Gregorio, where is he? He shot and killed Kai. We, Tina and myself, informed the Cannings, Gregorio and Raquel, that the Fabergé Egg they purchased was a counterfeit. Turns out they were aware of it. They forced us at gunpoint to come here."

"Why?"

"To eliminate us as witnesses. Kai. He tried to protect us. Raquel slipped on his blood."

"She slipped?"

"And the Domino Lady. They tried to kill her. She had the Egg."

"They?"

"Raquel had a gun too. Gregorio shot Kai. Raquel tried to kill the Domino Lady. She slipped on Kai's blood. After Gregorio shot him."

Lt. Brown nodded and opened his notebook.

Tina related a similar series of events to Lt. Brown. Lisa's account wasn't verbatim so he knew it wasn't pre-arranged. Lisa's description had enough of the key points to corroborate Tina's side of things. Enough of the details matched for his satisfaction.

However, Gregorio's version didn't match theirs.

"What about Gregorio?" Lisa asked.

"We'll be in touch," he said abruptly.

A bald, somber man in a similar suit tapped Lieutenant Brown on the shoulder.

"David, he wants a lawyer," he said in a stage whisper.

"Screw him. Let's take that asshole downtown," the sandy-haired lieutenant twitching his head.

He flipped his notebook shut and hoofed away to the locker room.

Lisa's head cleared.

The locker room doors slammed open. The lieutenant and his somber colleague pushed a red-faced Gregorio through.

"The Domino Lady killed Kai!" he cried with actual tears in his eyes.

The discord squelched the exact words he shouted. No one except Lisa paid attention.

In a surprise burst of energy, Gregorio jerked away from the two lieutenants. Unhandcuffed, he sprung away easily. He headed toward the door only to see two police officers blocking his way. Campus security glared at him. The two lieutenants edged toward the man with a desperate look in his eye. Various other police officers sensing something was wrong followed their lead.

Gregorio scooped up his pistol. It remained undisturbed in an attempt to preserve the crime scene.

"Let me out of here," he screamed as he circled the room with the gun.

The officers and the lieutenants stopped closing in on him.

With, one swift, fluid motion, Lisa seized her foil and stuck Gregorio in the back of his hand. The jab caused Gregorio's grip to naturally release causing the gun to drop.

Before it hit the mat, police officers tackled Gregorio. Lt. Brown cuffed the killer's hands as he gasped for breath underneath the weight of three policemen.

The bald lieutenant tipped his fedora in appreciation to Lisa. Lisa saluted with the blade in return.

This time the patrolmen dragged Gregorio out of the gym. They yanked him down the stairs, through the halls, and outside.

Lisa trailed behind the trio. She still clutched the foil just in case she had another opportunity to strike Gregorio resulting in a more deadly effect.

The humid temperature alerted Lisa that she was beyond the Hearst Gymnasium confines. She became aware of a surrounding crowd. Her friends were among them.

Tina returned to Lisa's side, pulling her away from questioning eyes. "Someone tipped off the police. That's how they're able to get here so quickly."

"How long have I been unconscious?"

"About an hour, you slipped and hit your head," Tina said.

Sporting a pony tail and pink lipstick, Ellen in her tennis shorts and blouse made a beeline to Tina and Lisa.

Tina smirked. "I'm glad you took my advice."

Changing the subject, Ellen asked, "How're you doing, Lisa?"

"How did you get past the police line?" Tina asked.

"I said I was here for my sister. I didn't say it was my sorority sister?" Ellen said conspiratorially. "Lisa, how're you doing? Raquel, Gregorio, and everything that happened up there."

Lisa began to tear up. The three women hugged and cried.

After several minutes, the emotional release allowed them to speak again.

"In case, you're wondering about me, the Domino Lady knocked me out," Tina shot a quick look at Ellen. A bruise on Tina's chin gave credence to her statement. "She removed Gregorio's money belt, wallet, and rings as well as absconding with Raquel's jewelry as well."

"The security guards outside reported the Lady Domino escaped. They had her trapped. But they didn't find any sign of her body. The only thing that they found was her bullet ridden cape," Ellen said.

She further explained that Officer Harvey, "a very cute young security guard" told her how the Domino Lady tossed the egg one way, threw her cape at his buddies, and rolled the opposite way of where she threw the egg.

"The security guards aren't good shots," Lisa added joking.

The joke only served to elicit tears. Lisa, Tina and Ellen hugged and cried again. They grieved the loss of a friend. They mourned the death of a protector. They lamented the criminal misdeeds to which they bore witness. They consoled each other until Lt. Brown cleared his throat.

"We need you to come with us to the President's House. The district attorney is already in possession of the counterfeit Egg. And Canning is trying to make a deal," he grunted.

The three women gazed upon the lieutenant with teary eyes.

His voice cracked. "Ahem. We need to collect the evidence there. Need you to confirm." He couldn't speak sensing their overwrought emotional state. He simply turned away. He held open the rear door to his cruiser for them.

Ellen, Lisa, and Tina crawled inside. They were driven away before they had to witness two still bodies in white sheets being hauled out of the building.

At the President's House, Tina and Lisa gathered and labeled the notes for the district attorney. Ellen identified the belongings of Gregorio, Raquel, and Kai.

Weary from assisting the police, the three hugged and cried some more. Then they all went home for a long, recuperative slumber.

The next evening Boynton offered a candlelight dinner at his apartment to help Ellen cope with the loss of her friend. Between sips of white wine, they compared notes of the day's events.

"The official statement from the University is the Domino Lady was involved. The security chief's a friend of mine. He told me that an anonymous phone call came in last night. Someone saw her enter the President's House. By the time, a security patrol arrived they witnessed her leaving the building," Boynton explained. "Her white gown attracted their attention; very careless of her, if you ask me. Naturally, the security guards gave chase and radioed for backup. More guards joined the pursuit all the way to the women's gymnasium. They were able to surround her. She told them not to come any closer or she'd destroy the Fabergé Egg. She's the one who stole it from the Library in the first place!"

"Oh, how thrilling!" Ellen squealed.

"Quite. The security guards had their guns drawn on her when she showed them the Egg. She knew she was trapped, so she tossed it over to them. One of them had the presence of mind to catch it. Then Miss Canfield came running out of the women's gymnasium screaming about a murder."

"Lisa told me that Tina yelled for help because that Chinese valet was shot by Gregorio and Raquel. He tried to protect Lisa and Tina," Ellen choked a bit in saying it. She mourned the loss of the man and his fighting skills.

"Canning has shown absolutely no remorse in that. Professor Brown and Miss Canfield were eyewitnesses to the murder. But the Domino Lady escaped. The only thing they found was her bullet-riddled cape," Philip said.

Ellen allowed him this moment to impress her.

"The fingerprints on the guns will be enough to convict Gregorio of murdering Kai along with their testimonies. Raquel has already paid for her part in the crimes," Ellen added.

"I'm sorry about your friend," Philip offered sincerely. "I had no idea she and her husband were involved with such corruption. An insurance detective is coming all the way from Hartford to investigate every one of the Cannings' insurance claims, past and present. This wasn't the only insurance scam they've pulled. Gregorio's already implicated several government custom officials and the 'expert' who verified the Egg's authenticity. He also named the forger who manufactured the counterfeit Egg for him."

"Miss Canfield's notes are very thorough in identifying it as a counterfeit. She informed the police that the Domino Lady returned with the Egg once she discovered it was a fake."

"Tina told the police that the Domino Lady forced her to lure the Cannings away from the President's House by claiming she stole the Egg. The Domino Lady ransacked the Cannings' belongings at University House. Took all their money and jewels."

Most of it will go to Kai's fiancé, Ellen thought.

Before the Domino Lady jumped out of the window at the President's House, she locked the pillow case filled with the Cannings' jewelry and money inside Kai's luggage. When Ellen returned with the police, she identified that only Raquel's and Gregorio's luggage had been ransacked. Since Kai's suitcase appeared to have been untouched, the police did not consider it as evidence. Ellen was able to collect and ship his personal effects to his fiancé, Jasmine. She included a note specifying who to contact to sell the jewelry. The note was compliments of the Domino Lady. Since Ellen already collected her share, what Jasmine did the remaining stash was no concern of hers.

"Ellen?" Boynton waved his hand in front of her eyes.

Blinking her long lashes to reveal sparkling caramel eyes, she re-focused on her anxious date and smiled.

"Could you still be suffering from shock?" he asked concerned.

"No, I mean, Yes. I'm fine. You were saying?" Ellen sighed.

"Lisa thinks the Domino Lady was going to blackmail them, the Cannings, that is, as well. But when the valet was murdered, that changed her plans," Philip theorized.

"That's enough about that awful Domino Lady," Ellen snapped with a gleam in her eye. "How about a more intimate discussion of your area of expertise, human biology?"

The End

A SOPHOMORE LIKE TALE

I have to admit that writing the Domino Lady tale I had to tap into my sophomoric side. In reading the six original tales, the sexual overtones were not lost on me. The action and mystery engaged my intellectual story telling. But the youthful (immature?) attitude that sex is a game was fun to play with. The Domino Lady's actions are not to be viewed as sexually demeaning. Remember she's in her twenties and all twenty-somethings are experts about everything.

GEORGE TACKES—After graduating college with an English degree in 1983, George wrote plays in the 1980s that were performed at Chicago theaters. From 1990s, he was a newspaper reporter for suburban newspapers.In the early 2000s, he worked as an associate editor for trade publications. After that, George married and started a family. The need to earn a profitable income surpassed writing ambitions. He entered the "exciting" world of IT support. In 2018, George attended his first Windy City Pulp and Paper Convention and got the pulp bug. In 2021, his first two stories appeared in Airship 27's Sherlock Holmes Consulting Detective #17. Also that year, Airship 27 published his first novel, "The Great Chicago Fire Conspiracy," which was nominated for Best Pulp Novel in 2021 by Pulp Factory. George lives in Oak Lawn, Illinois, with his wife, his daughter, and a very demanding dachshund named Bailey.

THE CONQUEROR'S THORN

By Gene Popa

The scents of orange blossoms and night-blooming jasmine wafted through the air on warm summer breezes, and mockingbirds were the only witnesses to one shadow that moved among others, silent through the tree-shrouded grounds, unerringly through darkness only feebly lit by the pale light of a quarter moon in the evening sky.

The figure made its way over a short stone wall and, trailed by the faint click of heels upon the pavement, stealthily ventured the fifty yards or so to a roadster parked at the end of the block. The driver's side door swung open, and the figure settled in behind the wheel. Having started the engine, the driver glanced up at the rear view mirror, and a pair of piercing brown eyes looked back.

A small smile crossed ruby red lips. Tonight wasn't a complete wash-out… she may not have gotten what she wanted, but at least she had helped herself to the contents of the open safe. From a pocket within her black cloak, she pulled three wrapped bundles of bills, each of them equaling a thousand dollars apiece. A third of that will go toward financing her continued efforts, while the remainder will be delivered anonymously, as always, to a carefully chosen charity.

If one were to have followed her trail to its point of origin, it would have taken them back over the wall, across the lawn, and up to a large and imposing mansion. One would have found an open window looking into the den of the house's master. And therein they would have seen an unmoving body, slumped in the chair behind the desk.

Upon examination, they would have discovered that the figure was not dead, but rather slumbering…albeit not naturally, but chemically. Those who knew him…or knew of him…would have identified him as McCallister by name. They would have known that he was a prominent importer of art, antiquities, and other rarities. A very select few would also have known that he dabbled as well in the importation and fencing of stolen goods, and very profitably so.

Mr. McCallister had found himself visited tonight by a figure shrouded in great mystery, demanding answers. The .22 caliber automatic trained on his chest prompted him to supply whatever information he could, although

83

it was not much. When he awakens in a few hours, he'll groggily recall being ordered to sit down, then the intruder having slipped behind him. A moment later, it felt as if a bee had stung the back of his neck, and then everything went instantly black. He'll assume a syringe with some sort of knock-out drug was used, but that's certainly preferable to the alternative…a bullet to the heart.

He'll also find the small calling card left in his now-empty safe, reading only…

Compliments of the Domino Lady

In Southern California, June days are much like one another…blue skies and sunshine from dawn to dusk. And so it was this bright Tuesday morning, as the sun beamed through the tall windows of an East-facing room of a stately home in the tony Holmby Hills neighborhood of Los Angeles. Although not as grand as the mansions of such well-known neighbors as Barbara Stanwyck and Jean Harlow, it is elegant enough. And its occupant, socialite Ellen Patrick, is considered by many to be as beautiful and vivacious as any of her Hollywood starlet neighbors.

But for those who are used to seeing the young blonde garbed in the latest in Paris fashions clinging to her shapely frame, the sight of her now might seem almost comical. Some would smirkingly ask if she enjoyed wearing men's pajamas. Very few among her party-hopping friends would know, or even much care, that the all-white garment she now wore is called a *gi*, and it is the uniform of a pupil of the ancient art of judo.

She bowed to a wizened old Asian gentleman, and he returned the gesture. And then, without warning, he lunged for her, attempting to seize her upper arms. In a blur of motion, the blonde grabbed the lapels of his own gi, and with a twist of her body, she deftly flung him over her hip and onto his back. Luckily, the floor was padded.

Impressively, he was back up on his feet in an instant, seemingly none the worse for wear. "Excellent, Miss Patrick," he said. "Soon, your skills shall prove the equal of my own meager knowledge, and there will be nothing more for me to teach you."

"That's bunk and you know, Sensei," Ellen replied as she walked over to a sideboard, picked up a small towel, and with it dabbed at the beads of sweat on her face. "You're the finest judoka master in America. If I can learn one-tenth of what you know, it would be a miracle…and it would take me ten years to do it!"

There was a long pause of silence, and then the slight and deceptively frail looking Oriental said, "Forgive this one for his impertinence, Miss Patrick.

Often, I am retained by women of means such as yourself to instruct them in the art of self-defense. Never have any of my pupils continued with their training beyond a lesson or two. I often hear the remark, 'This is harder than I thought it would be'. But not you. You have met with me twice every week for months now, and you have displayed true *kenshin*…a great enthusiasm for the art of judo. If I can be so bold, may I ask…why?" His face was impassive, and he spoke his inquiry in the most casual of tones. But his eyes were watchful, as if searching for some gesture of motion that would lend credence or suggest deceit from whatever she said in reply.

With a smile, the young woman removed a pin from her hair and shook her head as her long golden mane fell free. "A girl meets a lot of mashers on the cocktail party circuit, Mr. Kano. When they get handsy, it's helpful to be able to put my own hands to work and teach them some manners. A lady must protect her virtues, after all."

"Hmmmm," the gray-haired gentleman murmured softly, before responding only with, "Yes, of course." If he thought there might be more to it than that, he kept his own counsel.

Ellen bade her instructor farewell, took a shower, and dressed in slacks and a tight-fitting pullover top for the day. Her maid served the usual breakfast of hardboiled eggs, bacon, and a champagne mimosa to give the morning a bit of sparkle. Afterward she had plans to play tennis with friends at their country club. In all respects, it seemed a typically languorous day for any of her social set of fellow debutantes. But it was only after the moon came up that Ellen Patrick pursued decidedly different diversions. That was when the Domino Lady prowled the darkened landscape.

But she then made a call to her friends and begged off of playing tennis. Next, having placed a second call, she had extended her regrets to a friend throwing a party tonight, explaining that she had a simply dreadful headache, and would be going straight to bed after dinner. But instead, she used her time that afternoon and evening to mull over the information she had managed to acquire about a mysterious new crime boss in Los Angeles, a shadowy figure known only as 'Magnus'.

Admittedly, what she knew wasn't much. More maddeningly still, there seemed to be no one in the underworld who knew much of anything about this Magnus, despite the fact that, after coming from seeming nowhere six months earlier, he had swiftly built a mobster regime that threatened to throw the delicately balanced L.A. underworld into chaos. And chaos always resulted in bloodshed, much of it among the innocent.

Ellen wasn't sure what she was going to do about Magnus, if and when she ever solved the mystery of his identity. But in the criminal life, knowledge was a valuable commodity. And if she ever should find herself at odds with this mysterious crimelord, she wanted to be armed with as much information as possible about him.

But information alone wasn't enough. Nor was the law. Ellen Patrick learned that in the most devastating way possible when her crusading father, the District Attorney, was murdered by corrupt forces with tentacles deep within the mob, big business, and even law enforcement itself, and those sinister figures saw to it that Owen Patrick's murder remained unsolved, and his battle against them abandoned. Realizing she could not count on the police and the courts to always administer justice, Ellen had adopted the identity of the Domino Lady so as to insinuate herself within the body of organized crime itself, and deal it death blows from within.

In the underworld, the Domino Lady was considered nearly as much of a mystery as this Magnus. Criminals considered her one of them, although more of the 'Robin Hood' variety. For the Domino Lady was known to target other criminals who, by some unproclaimed code of her own, crossed lines and committed acts she deemed unacceptable. And while her gun had been known to turn its fury on a few, she preferred to incapacitate her victims, rather than kill them. The end result was usually that her targets were relieved of money or other precious items by the masked mystery woman.

And that, of course, was only partially the truth...the part which the Domino Lady herself allowed to be revealed. For it served her purposes that the underworld considered her one of their own. It allowed her to move amongst them more freely. If criminals knew she was in fact determined to put a stop to them all, the underworld would turn its full might upon her. No, it was far better to be thought of as a member of their wicked little fraternity, the easier to strike from its very heart of darkness.

And this role she played was abetted, albeit reluctantly, by the Los Angeles Police Department. Few cops could handle the bruising to their egos of having it known that some dame outwitted them and brought down so many major criminal figures, so they saw to it that virtually all mentions of her are kept out of the newspapers. And that had suited the Domino Lady just fine; being tabloid fodder could only increase the risk of her true identity being uncovered.

When she felt it necessary to turn someone over to the police, she would place an anonymous phone call, and then made certain enough evidence was found on the scene for the District Attorney to make a case stick. Thus, she was only a whispered rumor in police precincts. The only tangible proof of her very existence were the cards she would leave behind, the better to enhance her reputation among those whom she wants to make an impression upon.

Now however, circumstances had taken an unexpected turn. For on the front page of the *L.A. Chronicle* was the banner headline:

"Mystery Woman Nabs Safecrackers"

The article breathlessly told of a beat cop responding to the sound of a gunshot inside the second story office of a stockbroker shortly after midnight…. right around the time that the Domino Lady had been taking care of her business the night before, in fact…and burst through the door to discover a masked woman leveling a pistol at two men, both of whom were well-known to the authorities as professional safecrackers. She said she had seen the officer walking down on the street though an open office window and fired a shot into the air so that the noise would draw his attention. When the stockbroker was reached at home by reporters, he admitted that there were some $10,000 in bonds secured in his safe.

Accompanying the police officer last night was a photographer for the *Chronicle*, who frequently joined with cops on their late night beats in order to catch crimes in the offing. He took a picture of the woman, which the paper included with the story. She was garbed in what the writer's account claimed was a clinging black dress, with a dark red satin cloak with white interior, red elbow-length opera gloves, and a mask of the same color over her eyes. Tucked into her brown hair over her left ear was a rose. She identified herself only as "The Red Rose".

The policeman instructed her to remain for questioning, but she replied that it wasn't against the law to stop a crime, and thus there was no reason for her to stay any longer. However, she said, the police could expect to see her again, and soon. And with that, she removed the rose from her hair and tossed it to the officer, and then she slipped out of the office and melted into the shadows of the hallway and departed the scene. The lone officer was unable to pursue her without leaving the burglars behind and risking their certain escape. The photographer reported that he attempted to follow her, but that she eluded him once she made her way down to the street.

Ellen set the paper down, and her brow furrowed. Other than this newcomer's color scheme and the nom de plume she had chosen, that was an uncomfortably close description of the Domino Lady. She worried that some underworld figures may mistakenly assume it is her, and turn up the heat on the Domino Lady in retaliation. Worse still, this Red Rose may inadvertently shoot and kill some innocent bystander, and that might so poison the waters that the Domino Lady could find in impossible herself to continue her work.

With any luck, she's just some bored deb looking for kicks, and once the adrenaline rush of this escapade faded, she'll hang up her mask and go back to whatever life she led during the daytime. But unless and until that happened, the Domino Lady would be keeping an eye out for the Red Rose.

The days that followed were much like the ones before it, at least while the sun shone. But as it set on many of them, rather than remain at home studying press clippings and trying to piece together the mystery of Magnus from the few scanty scraps of underworld information she had managed to pick up, Ellen had taken a more direct approach.

The Domino Lady went on the prowl, shaking down informants, following leads, but time and time again finding herself at a dead end. Finally she realized that she needed a source that was wired into a higher level of crime, although pursuing it could be risky. Still, she decided she simply had no other choice. And after making some discreet inquiries, she learned just where her target would be that very night.

The femme fatale who stepped out that evening was Ellen Patrick, but the Domino Lady was never far behind.

She hadn't been on the guest list for this particular party, but a beautiful woman of means rarely has any trouble securing an invitation if she asked in just the right way, and so it was that Ellen mingled with the other guests, sipping her champagne, and keeping an eye on one attendee in particular.

"Gentleman" James Pendleton was an attorney who had lucratively specialized in representing criminal defendants...or, in the parlance of his clients, he's a mob mouthpiece. But unlike the typical low rent shysters, Gentleman Jim moved in a more rarefied atmosphere of wealth and influence. If you were a gangster facing hard time, and you could afford him, you hired Pendleton as your lawyer. If you did, odds are you'd either land a much less severe sentence, or potentially even walk away scot free.

And now, Ellen had watched as he stepped away from the party and went out into the landscaped floral garden to enjoy a cigar...alone. This was the moment she had been waiting for. She excused herself..."Must powder my nose"...from the ardent attentions of a young fellow who somehow felt he was impressing her by regaling the socialite with lengthy recitations of his past college gridiron achievements. Slipping outside into the darkness, she had crept over to some bushes on the opposite side of the mansion, where she had previously planted a leather satchel, inside of which contained the trapping of the Domino Lady. She stripped out of Ellen Patrick's evening gown and donned the raiment of her alter ego.

Then, having moved stealthily through the darkened scenery…something she had grown quite adept at…she quietly approached the lone figure standing in the shadowy garden, until she was no more than ten feet behind him. Standing there alone with his thoughts, a wisp of smoke curling up into the air from his Havana, he had no idea she was there until she chose to make her presence known. "Good evening, Counsellor," she said in a feminine yet firm voice.

Pendleton didn't jump in surprise, nor wheel around. Instead he casually turned to face the source of that voice. Even when, from the pale light provided from a few decorative electric lanterns placed around the garden, he spotted the pistol in her hand that was leveled directly at him, his face remained unperturbed. With a small but decidedly wry smile on his lips, he said casually, "If you intend to do any real damage, don't go for my heart…aim for my wallet instead."

Damn, he is a smooth one, the Domino Lady thought to herself. She returned his smile as she holstered her pistol, allowing a generous glimpse of her thigh as she did so. "That was only to keep you from shouting for help," she said. "Oh? And will I need any help?" he inquired, followed by a long drag on his cigar.

"I have a few questions," was her reply. "First, do you know who I am?"

"I'd be a poor servant of the honest people if I didn't know who the entrancing Domino Lady is," he lightheartedly offered. "And, if I may say so, in this starlight you are even lovelier than I had ever anticipated."

"Save the charm for another time, Mr. Pendleton," she responded. "And as for 'honest people', you and I both know that very few of them pass through your doorway."

Tapping the ash from his cigar to the ground, Pendleton asked, "Am I to assume that you're in need of something other than legal services from me? After all, these are hardly my office hours."

"What do you know about Magnus?" is all that she said.

For the first time he betrayed the slightest hint of surprise, as his left eyebrow arched just ever so much. "Now that is a very interesting subject," he replied. "*In brevi*…not much. *Ad longitudinem*…not a great deal more. He's quite the enigma, isn't he?"

"You're sure it's a he?" the masked maiden interjected.

"Oh yes," Pendleton responded. "Although his identity remains unknown, those who have communicated with him say for certain that he is a fellow. Not that I'm dismissing the possibility of a female accomplishing what he thus far has…particularly a beautiful and ingenious woman, with an enchanting pair of…"

"Careful, Counsellor…"

"…eyes behind that mask, which frankly I don't much care for, as it covers far too much of your lovely face."

"We're drifting off-topic, Mr. Pendleton," the Domino Lady gently admonished. "Just how does someone contact him?"

Sighing over his flirtations being so determinedly rebuffed, Pendleton said, "As I understand it, no one is able to reach him…he calls them. He sets up a specific day and time, and like clockwork rings them up to provide instructions and gather information. But I imagine you already knew that, courtesy of your visit with McAllister a short while back."

"You heard about that, eh?" she responded.

"Mr. McAllister is a client of mine," came the reply. "I trust you'll appreciate how I'm denting attorney/client privilege by having this conversation with you."

The Domino Lady gave him a small smiled pursed upon her red lips and said, "Duly noted, Counselor. Now then, how has Magnus been able to build his organization so quickly, particularly if no one knows who he really is?"

The lawyer rubbed his chin and furrowed his brow. "Whoever he is, he knows the Los Angeles underworld thoroughly. He carefully and explicitly reached out to specific men, each of them young, bold and hungry. They knew it would take them years to work their way up the leadership hierarchy of their respective 'families', but now Magnus is offering them an opportunity to achieve wealth and power much more quickly."

"Promises mean nothing to men like that," she rejoined. "What did he have to offer them beyond words? What can he actually deliver?"

"Ahh, but here we discover his true talent," Pendleton said as he grandly waved his hand through the air, as if he were enacting his final summation before a jury, the burning tip of his cigar leaving a faint glowing trail through the darkness. "Our Mr. Magnus would seem to be quite the criminal mastermind. He concocted a series of daring…and highly profitable…heists, and gifted the details of one to each of the men he contacted. They were free to enact his plans or not, and if they did, they were allowed to keep the full proceeds of their efforts. But…", here the attorney gestured with his index finger, and paused for dramatic effect before continuing. "If they wished to avail themselves of his further guidance, they had to join his organization, and kick back twenty percent of their gains to him. Apparently, it goes into a dummy bank account, and then filters through enough false front identities that no one is able to track it all the way back to Magnus. Or so I'm told."

Taking another puff on his cigar, the attorney added, "He certainly has grand ambitions. That's obvious enough from the name he's chosen."

"Promises mean nothing to men like that."

Somewhat perplexed, the Domino Lady asked, "What makes you say that?"

"Why my dear," came the reply with a chuckle. "Haven't you read your Plutarch? Magnus is the name that the Greeks gave to Alexander the Great!"

"So, he has delusions of grandeur," the masked woman mused. "Well, you've been very helpful indeed, Counsellor. Thank you."

"If I might offer one more piece of very pertinent information, dear lady?" Pendleton interjected. "I don't know the reasons why you are so interested in this Magnus, although I'm certain they are very good ones...and perhaps more imperative than even you suspect. The word is, he's been asking a great deal about you as well, and reportedly told one of his confederates that he has already taken steps to remove you as a potential threat to him. I simply felt you'd care to know that."

The attorney stepped forward, drawing closer to the masked blonde. She looked up and saw his Romanesque nose, his chiseled jaw and cheekbones, the distinguished strands of silver at his temples, and above all, his steel gray eyes, and for the barest of moments she imagined herself in his arms. Then she collected herself, and said, "Again, you have my thanks."

Reaching into his dinner jacket, Pendleton produced a small card and pressed it into the gloved hand of the Domino Lady. "My private number," he said in a soft voice. "Should you ever find yourself in need of a lawyer...or if you wish to exchange *information* again."

She smiled, turned, and walked back into the darkness of night. Making her way back around the grounds, she changed her clothing again, and Ellen Patrick rejoined the party just long enough to say her farewells and depart. As she left, she caught sight of Pendleton, who had also returned indoors, and was chatting up some lovely young debutante. Ellen sighed; it would be an easy thing to be swept up by the mesmerizing eyes and honeyed words of Gentleman James, but a dangerous path to follow, as he no doubt would be quite willing to share secrets about the Domino Lady to the right person, if it proved an advantage to him or one of his less-than-reputable clients. No, best to just leave things be with this one.

Still, she would keep his card...just in case.

Piloting her convertible through the darkened streets toward home, Ellen wondered what Magnus meant when he said he had taken steps to remove her as a threat? She knew that word would filter back to him that she was shaking down gangland for details on the mystery crimelord, but she had hoped he would assume that meant the Domino Lady was gathering information in anticipation of approaching Magnus about working together, or at the very least offering some other agreement that might avoid confrontation. Did he instead think she was preparing to try and strike against him for her own criminal ambitions? Or did he always plan to eliminate her as a latent danger, no matter what she did?

Most perplexing of all, what kind of "steps" could be taken to strike at her? It isn't as if the Domino Lady is easy to find, much less set a trap for.

Quite suddenly, uncovering the mystery of Magnus took on a much grimmer importance.

But while Ellen Patrick retired for the evening to further ponder what she had learned and decide her next course of action, another femme fatale kept busy in the shrouded streets of Los Angeles.

It was to be an easy job for Vinnie Mahone, a low rent hood who made money on the side as an arsonist-for-hire. He'd been paid to torch a building in the Boyle Heights part of town. Maybe it was for insurance money, maybe it was a shakedown…Mahone didn't need to know, so he didn't ask. The guy who wanted it done wasn't the talkative type anyway. He came up to the bar at Maxie's, the collar of his trench coat turned up, and with a fedora pulled down to partially obscure his face. He knew exactly who to go to, however; he stood next to Mahone, and without a word slid an envelope across the scuffed up bar, inside of which was $200 and a scrap of paper with an address on it. Also written on the note was a very specific instruction: *It burns tonight at 1:00 AM.* He then turned around and wordlessly walked out of the tavern.

Vinnie had been sorely tempted to take his sudden windfall and celebrate with some top shelf liquor, but then he wisely thought better of it. He'd need his wits about him if he was going to pull off the job right, and if he did do it properly, there was always the hope of further profitable opportunities from this silent benefactor.

As the clock neared the One AM hour, Mahone had already staked out the property. It was a single story building that housed three small businesses, which collectively represented the ethnic makeup of Boyle Heights: a Mexican tailor, a Jewish shoemaker, and a Russian tobacconist. There were no apartments in the building, so that meant that no one lived there. That pleased Mahone; not that he was squeamish about offing someone, but rather he would have charged more than two-hundred bucks for a murder job.

It was an old building, meaning it would have been plenty simple to crowbar open the aging back doors of each business, spread gasoline from the can he had brought along inside of each, and set the whole place up from one end to the other. A place this old, it'll be ablaze in no time.

The money man was very specific about the time, so Vinnie wasn't going to disappoint him. At five minutes to the top of the hour, Mahone wedged the notched end of his crowbar between the first wooden door and the frame, and was just about to pop the flimsy lock, when he heard a decidedly feminine voice from behind. "Excuse me fellah, but do you know where a lady could get a light?" Startled, he whirled around, brandishing the steel crowbar in his hand like a club, ready to strike at the speaker.

He was taken aback by the vision that faced him. Her curvaceous body was clad in silken black, with a dark crimson cloak over her shoulders. Behind her left ear was tucked a rose, and she wore a mask like kids do on Halloween over her eyes. In the single yellowed overhead light of the alleyway, she seemed almost radiant.

That's when Mahone finally noticed the small automatic pistol in her hand. He gasped and took a step back, his eyes widening fearfully. But she then astonished him by slipping the gun into a holster strapped to her right thigh beneath her slit skirt. "You're not worth wasting a perfectly good bullet on," she said. "A long stay in the state pen is what you really deserve." He hadn't noticed her hand next having reached inside the interior of her cloak.

"Ya stupid broad!" Mahone snarled, eyes that had a moment before been filled with fear now narrowed into a murderous glower. He jumped forward and raised the crowbar, prepared to send it smashing down across her skull. But instead of recoiling, she surprised him by swiftly stepping up closer to him. The bar swung past her head, missed by inches in a blur of motion. She pulled her right hand out from beneath her cloak and, holding something tight within the palm of her closed fist, she slammed her hand down onto the back of his neck. An instant later, the would-be arsonist gave a whine and crumpled to his knees, dropping the crowbar to the ground with a clatter, and as she stepped aside, he then collapsed face-first to the concrete alleyway, where he lay unmoving save for the noise of his breathing, and the unmistakable sound of…snoring.

The Red Rose returned the hypodermic syringe to the small pocket within her cloak. She plucked the flower from her hair and tossed it down, where it landed and remained on the back of the slumbering Mahone. She then turned and strode down the empty alley, cloak billowed behind her, accompanied only by the sound of the clack of her heels on the pavement. She made her way a block over, where she knew there was a police call box. One needed a special key to open the metal door of the small box mounted on a telephone pole, and those had to be formally requested from the police department, and the LAPD was quite choosey about who they allowed to have those keys. But the Red Rose had her means, and that included, naturally enough, the very key needed to access the phone. She picked up the receiver, and was connected with police dispatch, explaining what they would find when they went to the alleyway behind a particular address in Boyle Heights. Given the slumbering figure's past criminal record, along with his fingerprints all over the tools of his arsonist trade, the cops would have plenty to stick on the fellow when they arrived. She pursed her crimson lips in a small smile of satisfaction as she thought about him waking up in a cell in a few hours, and wondering just how the hell this "broad" landed him in the slammer.

Ellen had slept fitfully that night. Magnus was proving to be a more baffling mystery than she had expected. What's more, the whole thing was starting to wound her pride. Since she had begun her career as the Domino Lady, she had enjoyed the battles of wits she had played with the criminal class, in no small part because the odds were generally far in her favor. Oh, there were many she had gone up against who were smart, clever and shrewd, but nevertheless she had repeatedly proven herself to be more than capable of outwitting them. Generally speaking, the average hood came ready to play craps, but the game was chess, and the Domino Lady was already several moves ahead of them.

Now, she had the growing feeling that Magnus had not only captured many of her own pawns already, but was preparing to move to checkmate her as well. And that was not a feeling that sat well with her.

She lingered unenthusiastically over her breakfast and leafed through the morning papers, when she finally picked up the *Chronicle*, and found another front page story about the Red Rose. That was starting to rankle a bit as well. Oh, she knew fully well why the authorities kept as tight of a lid as possible on news coverage of the Domino Lady. But no one at City Hall or the Police Department seemed the least bit unhappy about how much attention this new masked marvel was getting, particularly in the *Chronicle*.

And it wasn't hard to understand why. The Domino Lady was a criminal, at least as far as the cops and the public knew. But the Red Rose was a genuine heroine…a do-gooder who was going above and beyond to make the streets of L.A. safer for all. Who wouldn't love a story like that? Hell, Warner Bros. would probably make a movie about her.

Yes, Los Angeles certainly seemed to love the Red Rose. *Maybe that's what I need to crack this nut*, Ellen thought to herself. People were responding positively to this new masked mystery woman, so she may well have gained sources of information that the Domino Lady herself can't access…and those sources may offer up more clues to just who Magnus is?

And it wouldn't hurt to have another pair of eyes watching her own back, if as she feared, Magnus wanted the Domino Lady dead. Yes, working with the Red Rose might well be the best hope of a solution to this puzzle.

Then again, that led to an entirely different mystery: just how was the Domino Lady supposed to even find the Red Rose? The odds of them simply crossing paths in the night were slim, at best. And at any rate, Ellen wouldn't want this other masked woman to get the drop on her by surprise in the dead of night. Again, the Domino Lady was a known felon, and the Red Rose might not wait for an explanation before putting a bullet in her! No, Ellen would have to be the one to approach her, and without posing any obvious threat to the Red Rose.

But again...*how*?

That's when she looked at the newspaper page again, and saw the photo of the police cuffing the man whom they claimed the Red Rose had incapacitated before he could burn a building down. All of the papers in Los Angeles carried stories about the Red Rose, but as far as Ellen could now recall, the *Chronicle* was the only one that usually got photos as well, including several of the lady herself before she disappeared into the night.

All of the big papers had photographers stringing along with the police overnight, but the *Chronicle* seemed to always be the lucky one who could get a shutterbug on the scene again and again. She confirmed this by asking her housekeeper, Consuela, to retrieve all of the local papers from the past few weeks, which covered the time since the Red Rose debuted. Ellen made a practice of saving the old newspapers for the local Boy Scout troop, which once a month would come by to take them for their paper drive.

She confirmed that her memory was correct...the *Chronicle* was the one paper that consistently got photos of either the Red Rose, or else the aftermath when the police arrived to pick up the pieces. What's more, the photo byline on each and every picture bore the same name: Nick Pagonis.

"Now that's too much of a coincidence to be a coincidence," the blonde said softly. There had to be some connection between this photographer and the Red Rose. And tonight, the Domino Lady would pay this Mr. Pagonis a visit, and discover for herself just what that relationship was.

It wasn't hard to find one Nikolas Pagonis in the telephone book, and as the sun was setting over the City of Angels, it was Ellen Patrick who drove her car along its darkening streets. But once night had fully arrived, it was the Domino Lady who stepped out of the vehicle.

She surreptitiously made her way up a fire escape on the rear of a seedy apartment building, reaching the third floor flat that she learned to be that of Pagonis. When she first committed herself to wearing a mask and undertaking this life, she made a point of paying attention to the little things, no matter how seemingly trivial at the time, and filing them away in her mind. And one of those myriad facts she had picked up along the way was that the newspaper photographers usually didn't hook up with police patrols until ten PM or so. After all, that's when L.A. only began to get really interesting. Therefore, she assumed that Pagonis would still be at home at that hour.

And she assumed correctly. Slipping through an open window into the darkened bedroom, she could hear movement in the next room. Her gloved hand grasped the doorknob and turned it, and the door quietly opened. She could see a man, almost certainly the man she was here to see, with his back to her, packing a shoulder bag with flash bulbs and camera film.

"Mr. Pagonis, pardon the intrusion," she said. The startled man spun around, and when he caught sight of her, his eyes widened in fear. "The…the Domino Lady?!? H-how did you…?" he stammered, unable to find the voice to continue speaking. He was a little less than average height, about 5'6", and slim, perhaps around forty-five years of age. He combed his thinning dark hair back, displaying a long forehead. He had the sharp nose and olive complexion so prevalent among Mediterranean peoples. He was in many respects a perfectly unpresuming man, someone you wouldn't pay much attention to if you passed him on the street.

"Please sir, I mean you no harm. You're in no danger from me," she spoke soothingly so as to calm him, raising both hands with the palms out, to show him she was not holding a weapon. The man trembled, sweat beaded on his brow, but his rapid breathing started to slow, and he seemed to be regaining his composure.

Pretty jittery for a crime scene shutterbug, the Domino Lady mused. In a reassuring voice, she said, "I only have a few questions I'd like to ask you. Would that be all right?"

"Shu…sure," he stammered.

She motioned with a nod and a gesture of her hand for him to take a seat at the dining table. She did likewise on the opposite side, hoping to put him at ease by assuming such an unthreatening position. Her eyes glanced around the room, and she was a bit surprised that a tabloid street photographer should have so many shelves packed with books…and not the expected dimestore detective novels, but volumes of a weightier variety, such as Voltaire and Von

Clausewitz. Her eyes then returned to him and met his twitchy gaze, and as they sat looking at one another, she gave a small smile, and then she spoke.

"I believe you have some sort of relationship with the woman known as the Red Rose, am I correct?"

He hid his shock poorly as his eyes widened and his lips parted as he took a sharp intake of breath. "Yeah…yeah, I do. I mean, kind of," he replied apprehensively.

"Tell me about it, and about her," the masked blonde said, crossing her hands on the table before her.

Pagonis gulped, and then responded, "I was on the beat with Officer Wysocki a couple of weeks back when we heard a gunshot, and saw someone waving him up from an office window. We ran up there, and found a woman, and a couple of jokers she had collared."

"Yes, I've read about that in the paper," the Domino Lady interjected. "Tell me how you came to have ties with her."

By now, the photographer seemed calmer, as if he finally realized the Domino Lady was being truthful when she said she wasn't there to harm him. His nerves steadied and his voice lost its tremor as he continued. "As Wysocki was cuffing the safecrackers, Red Rose took a powder, but I went after her. I told everybody later that she got away from me, but actually I caught up to her down on the street. I told her we could help each other. Guy in my line of work, I pick up a lot of tips, which I usually pass on to the cops, but I told her maybe if I heard something I thought she'd be interested in, I could tell her instead."

"And what's in it for you, Mr. Pagonis?" she queried.

"I get first coverage of her. My editor is thrilled with this whole masked crimefighter angle, and he's paying me a bonus for every shot I get, either of her, or the mugs she busts."

Looking him directly in the eyes, the blonde asked, "Do you know who she really is beneath that mask?"

"No," he replied firmly. "And even if I did, I wouldn't tell you."

"Good. I admire integrity," she said with a smile. "But tell me this, how do you communicate with her?"

"I gave her my number, and every day she calls and asks me if I've got anything. I don't know where she's calling me from," Pagonis added, to emphasis the fact that he couldn't give up any details of her real identity even if he wanted to.

To the Domino Lady's inquiry of, "Did you have anything for her tonight?" the reply was, "No, things are pretty quiet today."

The blonde pushed her chair away from the table, the legs squealing across the worn wooden floor, and she stood up. "When she calls you tomorrow, please tell her that the Domino Lady very urgently wants to meet with her. Set it up for tomorrow night. Let her choose the place and time, so that she's completely at ease, and will know that this isn't any sort of a ruse on my part. You can come along if that's what she wants, Mr. Pagonis. And who knows, when all is said and done, you may just have yourself a major exclusive story."

As she turned and walked toward the bedroom, the Domino Lady looked over her shoulder and added, "I'll call you by 9:00 PM tomorrow for the details." And with that she stepped into the darkness of the second room, slipped back out through the window, and swiftly yet noiselessly made her way down the fire escape, her dark cloak fluttering behind her. Back on the ground, she melted into the night. A minute later, a pair of headlights winked on, and an automobile rolled through the grimy alleyway and out onto the street, and then sped away into the starlit nighttime.

She was steering the car back toward Ellen Patrick's home when she got to thinking. It was still early, after all, and she was dressed for business, as it were. Maybe she ought to go out and see if she could stir up a little adventure?

She was fresh out of leads about Magnus, but there might be other fish to fry. The *Chronicle's* crime photographer wasn't the only one who picked up the occasional tip. From chatter she had overheard at an off-the-books speakeasy that the criminal element...including the Domino Lady...frequents, a couple of breaking-and-entering guys had been casing the house of a well-to-do couple who had sailed for Hawaii that very afternoon, leaving their home unattended. And within that home were supposedly art, antiques and jewelry that would fetch a fine sum from any fence worth his salt.

She had intended to phone an anonymous tip to the police to thwart the theft, but now she deliberated taking a more personal interest in it. Her mind finally made up, a wry half-smile graced her lips, and she piloted the car toward the house in question.

Three hours later she was quietly standing shrouded in the darkness of the recessed doorway of the carriage house, which gave her an unobstructed view of the entire back of the home. From what she had picked up at the bar, the owners had no live-in servants, so the place sat empty, making it ripe for the picking. The blonde felt a sudden shiver and she pulled her black cloak more tightly around her. It may be summer in Los Angeles, but the ocean breeze still brought a chill to the night air. She reflected on the fact that her filmy attire wasn't well-suited for stakeouts. Truthfully, she was garbed more as a means

She piloted the car toward the house in question.

of distracting a male opponent, giving her a vital edge in situations where seconds count. Being out in the elements for hours on end was another thing entirely.

Plus, she was bored. Standing silently in the dark listening to crickets and night owls for what seemed like an eternity, she began questioning the wisdom of even doing this. *What if those clowns don't pick tonight to strike? What if they already came and went, and she was waiting out* there *for nothing?* She felt another shiver, and she asked herself, *How in the world does the Red Rose do this sort of thing?*

It was just then that she caught sight of two shadowy figures approaching the back door of the house. Her eyes were well accustomed to the gloom by now, and she watched as one of them took something from his inside coat pocket, fiddled with the doorknob for a good ten seconds, and then suddenly the door swung open. The two men looked around one last time to make certain they were unobserved, not realizing that in fact a pair of eyes hidden in the blackness were riveted on them. They then slipped quietly into the house.

Emerging from her hiding place, the Domino Lady carefully approached the house, placed her hand on the now unlocked knob, and gently pushed the door, which opened silently on well-oiled hinges. She entered the house, and slowly moved through the darkened room, taking great care to stay quiet and not betray her presence. Luckily, her eyes were well-attuned to the darkness, and with the faint moonlight that streamed in through the windows, she was able to make her way.

Moving from what she discerned was a mud room into a hallway; she was pleased to discover a rug beneath her feet, which would muffle the click of her heels on a hardwood floor. Suddenly she heard voices up ahead, and as she journeyed down the long hallway, she finally came to an open doorway.

Cautiously peering in, she saw the two intruders in the living room. They had drawn the curtains so that they could use their flashlights without fear of being seen by anyone outside through the windows. One of them removed a painting from over the mantle, broke the frame, and quickly rolled the canvas up and placed it inside a leather satchel. The other took a pair of figurines from a shelf, carefully wrapped each in cloth, and then placed both bundles in the satchel as well.

One of them then said, "I'm going into the den to crack the safe, you finish up in here." He then exited the room through another entryway on the opposite side from where the Domino Lady was. Good, that left her with only one to deal with.

Stealth was what was required now, so she carefully removed the syringe from its pocket inside of her cloak and crept up behind the figure who was busily placing silver candlesticks into his bag. In one deft motion she plunged the needle into the side of his neck, and the powerful sedative that coursed through his bloodstream instantly robbed him of consciousness. Moving as quickly as she could, she wrapped her arms around his chest from behind in order to gently lay him on the floor, so that his collapse didn't create enough noise to alert his partner.

However, his flashlight fell from his hand and clanged to the floor. She knelt down to grab it and switched it off, and in so doing placed herself in the torch's beam of light, illuminating her.

Who knows why the other burglar chose that moment to return to the room, but he did. Spotting the masked woman in the light, he let out a loud grunt that was part surprise and part anger, and his right hand slipped inside of his coat, emerging a moment later with a .38 firmly in his grasp. Even as the Domino Lady sprang from her crouched position and threw herself behind the back of a chintz sofa, he began squeezing the trigger and fired rounds at her. She heard one of them whiz uncomfortably close by her head.

She pulled her own pistol from its garter belt holster and held her breath as she waited to make certain he had ceased firing. With any luck, he thought he had hit her, and his guard was down. After several moments in which the only sound she could hear was the throb of her own fast-beating heart, she suddenly sprang up from behind the couch, instantly leveled her pistol toward where her assailant had stood, using her other hand to steady her aim.

But he was no longer there. In fact, she couldn't see him anywhere in the darkened room.

He must have gone back through the other door, and was elsewhere in the house. Or was he hiding just outside the entryway, waiting for some sign that she had come out into the open, so that he could resume shooting at her? And then again, there was also the possibility he was making his way down the long hallway, and would emerge through the open doorway that was behind her, which would leave her completely exposed.

She strained to hear any sound that might give her some clue. Suddenly she heard the creak of a floorboard, but she couldn't discern exactly where it came from. Her heart raced and her skin started to dampen with perspiration, and she could feel a sense of panic that started to well up within her. This had gone terribly wrong! She came into this without a plan, and had blundered into a veritable shooting gallery...with herself as the target!

The houses in this neighborhood were set far enough apart that almost certainly none of the neighbors heard the gunshots and called the police, so the blonde could not count on the cavalry in blue rushing to her rescue. And she hadn't noticed a telephone, so she couldn't call for the cops herself. Her only hope, she reasoned, was to make her way back to the outside door and get away…hopefully without bumping into the gunman.

But then she paused, taking a deep breath and holding it in, as her meditation studies had taught her so as to calm herself. What would escaping accomplish, beyond not getting shot? Yes, that's the most important thing, but it would also mean her efforts here tonight would be wasted. No, she couldn't just up and run away.

She thought through the situation. She and the gunman were in a game of cat and mouse. The darkness both helped and hindered each equally; he was as blind in the dark as she was, but he couldn't risk using his torch or turning on a light switch, for risk of exposing his position.

She had been the prey and he the predator, but now she needed to reverse their positions. Ironically, the only way to do so would be to make herself the bait to trap him.

Cautiously she stepped out from behind the sofa, pistol ready in her grip as she carefully made her way back to the open doorway she had first entered through. She peered around the corner, making certain her adversary wasn't lurking there, and was relieved to find no sign of him in the immediate area.

She began to move slowly through the dark hallway, alert for the slightest movement, the simplest sound. There wasn't the barest sign of life, other than her own…yet she knew he was there someplace in the darkness, as anxious to find her as she was him.

As she moved forward, her foot came down upon a loose floorboard beneath the rug, and it gave the slightest of groans. But it was enough to betray where she was…and as she discovered an instant later, her quarry was only a few feet away from her in the inky shadows. He gave a surprised gasp as he spun around toward the source of the sound and fired a bullet. Having heard the rustle of his clothes and his sudden exhalation, the Domino Lady's instincts told her to throw herself to the side, and that is what saved her from taking the slug.

However, unseen by the blonde, there was sideboard along that part of the hallway wall, and she had slammed hard against it with her hip and wrist, and the sudden jolt of pain caused her to drop her gun to the floor. Instinctively the Domino Lady lashed out with her left leg, hoping to strike her nearby assailant and ward him off for a few moments, until with a bit of luck she could recover her weapon. Fate was with her, and her foot kicked the gun hand of the intruder, knocking the pistol from his grip and sending it skittering across the floor.

But although disarmed, he was far from helpless. With a growl he blindly threw out his left arm in the direction of the figure who had struck him, and the back of his meaty hand smashed across the side of the Domino Lady's head, sending her reeling with a pained moan. She dropped to her knees, momentarily dazed from the blow. After a shake of her head, she struggled to get back up to her feet...but then found arms reaching around her from behind. One hand clamped hard around her left wrist, while the other arm snaked its way across her throat.

"Yeah, I thought you were a dame when I saw yah in the light," her attacker growled, his hot breath in her ear. "I think I saw a mask on yah, too. So I'm guessing you're that Red Rose broad. I dunno how yah found out we'd be hittin' this joint tonight, and I dunno what yah did with Mel. But you'n me are gonna have a little fun, cutie...until I wring that pretty neck of yours, that is!" He gave a harsh guffaw to punctuate his crudely lethal threat.

But while he believed he was in complete control of the situation, the Domino Lady calmly and coolly planned to turn the tables. She began by lifting her right foot, and then slammed it down atop his as hard as she could. And despite the leather of his shoes, the heel of her own shoe drove down like a railroad spike, causing him to give a loud bark of pain and, more importantly, loosen his grip on her.

She then swiftly followed up by balling her right fist and throwing it up and backward over her shoulder, perfectly approximating where his nose should be. She felt the cartilage flatten from the blow, and he gave an anguished moan. His hand released her wrist and his arm slipped loose from across her throat, and in an instant she gripped his right arm with both hands and expertly flipped him over her shoulder. He landed flat on his back with a thud and a groan, but within moments was sitting up...precisely as she had expected.

She had a vial filled with more knockout serum in her cloak, but she knew she didn't have even the few seconds needed to spare to fill her syringe before he would be up and enraged and on the attack once more. So, she improvised.

With a deft move she peeled the long opera glove from her left arm, twisted either end around each of her hands, and dropped to one knee behind him. She pressed her other knee against his spine to hold him in place as he sat upright on the floor. And then she wrapped the glove around his throat, using the makeshift garrote to strangle him.

He gurgled and gasped, as his hands clutched frantically at the fabric wrapped tight across his windpipe, and his feet kicked at the floor. Relentlessly, the blonde pulled the noose as tightly as she could, robbing him of the vital oxygen his burning lungs begged for.

Steadily his movements grew more sluggish, until at last his arms fell limply to his sides, and save for some spasmodic twitches of his left leg, he was still. Another few moments of this, and he would be dead.

Except that the Domino Lady never killed unless given no other choice. Having rendered him unconscious and no longer a threat, she ceased choking him. She pushed the now senseless burglar, who gulped in air with great heaving sounds, from her knee and onto his side, where he laid unmoving. It was only then that the enormity of the moment struck her, and she let out the breath she had held the entire time in a large whoosh.

She struggled back up to her feet, and the Domino Lady moved closer to the wall and leaned against it, as a tremble of both relief and excitement raced through her body. This had been the closest she had come to dying since she had first placed the mask upon her face, but she found that she wasn't afraid. She had faced the challenge and she had overcome it by her wits and her skills.

All the same, it wasn't an experience she was eager to repeat again anytime soon. She would leave the role of dark avenger skulking in the shadows to the Red Rose…or any of the other masked vigilantes in New York and Chicago she'd heard rumors about. If this little escapade proved anything, it was that the Domino Lady worked best in her own way, choosing her own battlefields and moments to strike.

With the two would-be thieves incapacitated at last, the blonde knew it was safe enough to turn a light on and locate a telephone. When that was accomplished, she placed a call…as an unnamed 'concerned citizen', of course…to the cops, telling them she saw burglars break into this address.

When a radio squad car pulled up on the street within minutes, and the pair of officers found the open rear door and entered inside with their guns drawn and ready, they discovered the dozing housebreakers, along with a card dropped beside one of them, announcing this as the work of the Domino Lady. And the lady in question was already speeding her way home, where she intended to immerse herself in a soothingly hot bubble bath.

She slept late that morning, but woke up refreshed, other than a few kinks from the grappling match she'd had the night before. Happily her masseuse was only a phone call away, and soon enough she was under the superb ministrations of his expert hands. As he kneaded her sore muscles, Ellen pondered her coming introduction to the Red Rose. If she was indeed more adept at taking the kind of proactive actions that weren't the Domino Lady's forte…as the previous evening demonstrated…she could be a valuable asset in the mission against Magnus, by coming at him from a different angle. The blonde hoped that squad room chatter about last night's escapade made its way to Pagonis, and that he shared it with the Red Rose. It would make their introduction easier if this new mystery woman recognized that the Domino

Lady also served the cause of justice.

The story was buried in the morning papers: police were tipped off to a home burglary, and found two intruders within, both unconscious, with signs of a struggle. Officials said they had no idea who had incapacitated the intruders. As she had expected, the cops still weren't going to admit the Domino Lady even existed, much less that she's thwarting crimes. L.A. only had room for one masked maiden at a time, it seemed. But that was okay…she had still managed to stop the theft, and she had the pleasure of making the confounded cops wonder just whose side she was really on anyway.

As she had promised, she dialed Nick Pagonis's number at the appointed hour, and he informed her that he had spoken with the Red Rose, and she was anxious to meet with the Domino Lady. The blonde would pick the photographer up at an appointed place and they would drive to the spot chosen by the other mystery woman, which Pagonis explained was an office building near downtown, to ensure privacy. Somehow or another, the Red Rose had access to the building.

The blonde avenger should have felt a sense of relief, knowing that she might at last have the means to get closer to solving the mystery of Magnus. But instead she felt apprehensive. Maybe last night's struggle was still preying on her mind. All she knew for certain was that she didn't want to walk into any more situations where she wasn't in control.

She made one last check of her accessories, making certain her pistol was loaded and the syringe was filled with knockout serum.

She threw her dark cloak over her shoulders and adjusted her mask as she looked herself over in a mirror, and then made her way to the garage. There, beneath a sheet to hide it from any prying eyes, was the black painted Ford supercharged V8 coupe that was the Domino Lady's mode of transportation. There was nothing unusual about it to distinguish it from any other models, so she was free to drive on city streets without attracting the undue notice of the police…unless of course any of them happened to peer into the darkened interior of the vehicle to see the driver. And if such an eventuality occurred, it would be a simple matter for the blonde to quickly pull off her mask and resume being Ellen Patrick, society girl.

She had seen to it that the car itself was untraceable to her. She had bought it under an assumed name, making the vehicle anonymous. Even the license plates were fakes; the Domino Lady knew an ex-con who had plenty of experience in the pen making plates, so she had paid him to create a couple just for her. These could be easily attached and removed from the vehicle by magnets attached to the back. Should a cop radio in a description of her auto along with its license number, once she got to some secluded spot, she could within moments replace the plates, and thus hide in plain sight.

After having opened the garage door, she pulled the sheet off of the vehicle and slipped behind the wheel. It rumbled to life and the car rolled smoothly out of the bay. She nimbly stepped out of the auto to close the door behind her, and moments later was cruising toward Pagonis's neighborhood.

He had named a corner where she could pick him up, which was out-of-the-way enough so as to not attract attention. She pulled up just before 10:30 in the evening, and the photographer opened the passenger side door and got in. "Brought your camera along, I see," the blonde commented, to which he replied, "Yeah, a force of habit. Besides, you hinted there might be a scoop for me in this, so I want to be ready if it comes."

The drive took a quarter of an hour, with little said between the two passengers. The Domino Lady was tempted to pump Pagonis for more information about the Red Rose, but she got the sense he wasn't too interested in saying anything more. Furthermore, she had to remind herself to be careful, for fear that in a bit of idle chatter; she may inadvertently say something which could give the cagey press photographer some clue to her real identity.

Soon enough they came to the nondescript four story office building on San Pedro St. The Domino Lady spotted an unattended all-night parking garage down the block and steered her car into it. At this time in this neighborhood, filled as it was with professional offices and no residences, there was no one who lingered nor passed by, so the Domino Lady and the photographer made their way unobserved down the sidewalk to the specific building they had come here to enter. Pagonis carried the tool of his trade, a Graflex Speed Graphic, in his right hand. The masked beauty couldn't help but notice that for all of his cool demeanor, the photographer had beads of sweat across his brow. She'd seen the same nervous perspiration when she confronted him in his apartment the night before.

Finally they reached the entryway to the building. "She said she'd leave it unlocked, and...presto!" Pagonis said as he pulled open the door. Inside was a small lobby, with a directory identifying all of the occupants. On the third floor was something called Argead Ltd. Pagonis pointed to the name and said, "That's it, come on."

They entered into the elevator car, closed the gate, and slowly began to rise. When they reached the third floor and stepped out of the lift, they stood in a dimly lit corridor. Moving as if he had some familiarity with the layout, Pagonis turned to the left and led the masked woman down the hall until they approached a particular door. The frosted glass was lettered ARGEAD LTD.

This door, too, was unlocked. Pagonis placed his hand on the knob, turned it, and the door opened with a small squeak of its hinges. "Ladies first," he said, and for the first time since she'd met him, the Domino Lady saw him smile. Given his dark, sharp features, it wasn't a comforting look.

She stepped into the room, which was as dimly lit as the outside hallway; the Domino Lady took quick stock of it. This was an outer reception area, with only a battered desk for a secretary, and a wooden chair behind it. Against the wall opposite the entry was another door, presumably to an office. This door was ajar, but the room beyond was pitch dark.

"Hello?" the Domino Lady said, as she heard the door behind her close. There was no other sound for the span of just a few moments, and then a figure from within the office opened the door wide and stood in the frame. Her shapely figure was garbed in a black dress, with her dark red satin cloak fastened across her upper breastbone and draped down her back. The mask across her eyes and the crimson flower in her dark hair finished the look.

And she held a small pistol in her right hand and aimed it directly at the Domino Lady.

"Did you honestly think I would fall for your little trick?" the Red Rose asked contemptuously.

"Please," the blonde crime-fighter said, as she mustered all the calmness in her voice that she could. "You misunderstand. This is no trick, and I only want to talk with you."

"You can do your talking to the police," the woman coolly said. "I've known for a while now that you've been stalking me, waiting for the chance to take me down before I got to you. Nick told me everything he had heard about it from his stoolies."

The Domino Lady spun her head sharply to her right to look at Pagonis, who through the corner of her eye she had seen move away from the doorway behind her and over to the side of the room. "What does she mean?" she demanded. "Why would you tell her that?"

He said nothing, but the Red Rose continued, "And when you came to see him last night, we realized this was the perfect opportunity to capture you and put an end to your little criminal antics." The Domino Lady turned her face to again look at the woman before her. It was like looking in a funhouse mirror in which everything is twisted into the opposite.

"Listen," she said, a sense of urgency now having crept into her voice. "If you'll just let me explain…" But the brunette cut her off by addressing Pagonis. "Nick, be sure to get a good shot of me and her now. It will make a great front page exclusive," she said as a small half-smile came to her ruby lips. Her gun was still pointed firmly at her target's chest, finger on the trigger.

"Now then, Domino Lady," the Red Rose said firmly. "If you'd be so kind as to carefully remove the pistol I know you're carrying and place it on the desk,

"Why would you tell her that?"

and then have a seat." With this, Pagonis took the wooden chair from behind the desk and placed it behind the Domino Lady. He stepped back to where he had been and raised his camera. "It really isn't an occasion to ask you two lovely ladies to smile," he said with a smirk, "but feel free to say cheese."

He lifted his camera up in order to take the shot, and the Domino Lady knew this was her only chance. She counted on the Red Rose dividing her attention between her and the movements of the photographer, so she grasped the hem of her own cloak and with a wide swing of her arm, swept the garment out. As it fluttered past the brunette's face, she reacted just as the Domino Lady hoped she would…she instinctively recoiled, and brought her left arm up to shield her face, which also conveniently blocked her view of the blonde.

Happily, the Red Rose didn't also reflexively pull the trigger. In a blur of motion, the Domino Lady threw a sweeping upward kick with her right leg, and her foot smashed up into the other woman's right wrist. The impact caused the Red Rose's hand to open and her gun to fall to the floor.

In the span of the barest of moments, Domino Lady calculated what her next move should be. She reasoned that she only had a second or two at most before the brunette recovered her senses and reacted. That did not give the Domino Lady enough time to draw her own gun from her thigh holster. Likewise, if she threw herself down on the floor to try and retrieve the Red Rose's own fallen pistol, it would leave her vulnerable to attack before she could turn the gun on the other woman. And anyway, she didn't want to hurt the woman, just calm the situation down…and then find out why Nick Pagonis had filled the Red Rose's ears with lies.

She elected to try and incapacitate Rose without harming her, so she grabbed for her left wrist, intending to twist her arm up behind her back in a hammer lock. But even as she did so, the Red Rose balled her right fist, and with viper speed slammed a punch across the Domino Lady's chin. The blow spun the stunned blonde sidewise and caused her to stagger a few steps before she could regain her footing.

Unfortunately, those few moments were all the brunette needed to go on the attack. Rather than risk the time it would take to try and retrieve her weapon, she lunged at the Domino Lady, pressing her hands to the other masked woman's shoulders and pushing her backward. The blonde let out a sharp gasp as she was shoved hard against the desk, her tailbone taking the brunt of the impact with the wooden edge.

As she continued to press her rival against the table, the Red Rose also bent the Domino Lady backward at the waist, until her shoulder blades were against the table top. The brunette then pressed her left forearm across the blonde's upper chest so as to keep her pinned down, while she drew her right arm back and made a fist.

"If I have to wallop you unconscious to settle you down, so be it!" the dark-haired crime-fighter snarled as she prepared to unleash a torrent of punches to the face of her adversary.

But the Domino Lady was not about to simply lay there and let this woman play Jack Dempsey on her pretty pan. A component of the art of judo is using your opponent's attire against them. That's no easy thing when the opponent in this instance had no sleeves or jacket lapels, and in fact was wearing a plunging neckline gown. But there was another garment that could be put to use by the blonde.

Throwing her hands up, the Domino Lady's fingers clutched at the Red Rose's mask, yanking and twisting it, so that in an instant it went from disguise to blindfold! Suddenly confused by being unable to see, the brunette was unprepared for her adversary to then roughly shove her away with her hands, and to follow up by lifting her right leg, placing the sole of her heeled shoe against the Red Rose's midsection, and pushing her backward with enough force that the brunette stumbled back on her own heels and nearly spilled to the floor before she could right herself. Only then was she able to readjust her mask.

That gave the Domino Lady the precious seconds she needed to launch a new offensive. She was done playing nice. If this ersatz doll was so damned intent on playing rough, the blonde was more than willing to show her what the original masked woman could do!

She started with a hip toss, which sent the Red Rose down hard to the floor, where she landed with a thud and a yelp. The brunette scrambled up to her feet as swiftly as she could and, with a growl of anger and frustration, threw herself at the Domino Lady. But the blonde deftly side-stepped her, using her billowing cloak to distract her charging opponent, much as a matador would with a bull. The brunette tumbled again to the floor.

As she got up off of her hands and knees and turned to face her opponent, the brunette's face was flushed red with fury. The Domino Lady said nothing; she merely assumed a slightly crouched stance and brought her open hands up in preparation.

It became clear to Domino Lady that her opponent had no knowledge of any martial art. But she was strong, and she definitely knew how to throw a punch. So Domino Lady had to avoid the Red Rose's fists at all costs; even better, she had to not let the brunette have any chances to swing at her at all.

With a roar of anger, the Red Rose flung herself once more at the blonde, and was upon her in an instant...or rather, the empty space where Domino Lady had been before she dropped to the floor with feline grace and swept her left leg out. She caught the brunette's own left ankle just as she stepped down. The inevitable result was that the startled masked woman was tripped and fell face-first to the wooden floor, which she hit hard, as evidenced by a pained groan.

Climbing back up to her feet, Domino Lady looked down at the figure that laid prostrate below her and said, "Now will you please calm down and listen to me? If I wanted you dead, you'd have a bullet in you right now."

But then another voice spoke, as Nick Pagonis, from behind the blonde, said, "How about that smile now, pretty lady?" The Domino Lady whirled around, prepared for some new attack. But she wasn't ready for what happened next.

Holding his camera up, Pagonis fired the flash. Her vision having been adjusted to the dim light of the office, the blonde was instantly blinded, seeing only fiery spots before her eyes.

It was then that Red Rose had recovered enough to get up on her knees and retrieve the syringe from her cloak, and with the hypodermic held tight in her hand, she plunged it forward. The Domino Lady felt the sharp sting of the steel needle effortlessly pierce the thin crepe fabric of her dress and stab into her derriere.

"Ohhhh nnnnnnnnn…" she muttered, even as she collapsed to the floor in a heap, utterly senseless.

"Smart thinking, Nick," the brunette said as she stood up. She rotated her right arm in a windmill motion as she rubbed her shoulder with her left hand, her face twisted into a small grimace as she winced in discomfort. "She's tougher than she looks," the woman continued.

"We're lucky you never gave her a chance to pull her piece," Pagonis replied.

"Yeah," Red Rose said in a detached voice. Yet a few moments later, there was much more vim in her tone as she asked, "But why was she so insistent on continuing to pretend she wasn't a threat to us?"

"Funny thing about that," the man said almost casually as he stepped behind the brunette. He pulled a sap from his jacket pocket, drew his arm back, and with a brutal swing smacked the blackjack against the base of her skull, making a dull thud as it struck. An instant later she was on the floor alongside the Domino Lady, and just as unconscious.

Wakefulness did not come gently. Rather it emerged with sudden flashes of semi-coherence. Her skull still felt as if it were stuffed with cotton, and her throat was dry.

When she could finally string a few orderly thoughts together, the first thing that came to mind was, *So...that's what that feels like.*

She heard herself make a soft moan, and then she lifted her head with no small effort. She blinked her eyes, but her vision was still too blurry to discern what she was looking at. Was someone standing in front of her?

Then there was another brilliant flash of light and the sound of a bulb popping. She winced and shut her eyes against the glare, but already it felt as is white needles had stabbed through her eyeballs into her brain.

"Thank you, my dear," came the voice. "I was right not to expect to recognize who you are under that mask, but I'll compare this photo with the picture archives at the *Chronicle.* Someone as pretty as you must have surely shown up on the society page at some point. I just need to know, you understand. I simply can't stand a mystery."

The visual shock from the camera flash helped speed the unclouding of her head, and her vision began to clear. She was in a different room than before. Given the desk and filled bookshelves, she guessed it was the inner office which Red Rose had emerged from earlier. How much earlier? The blonde had no sense of how long she had been unconscious, but it was still night outside the windows. If the brunette's knock-out serum was anything like her own, the effect should have lasted no more than a few hours.

She tilted her head to look more closely at the desk, and on it saw her mask, and alongside of it both her and Red Rose's pistols. She would be concerned that he might uncover her real identity, if not for the fact that she was certain he didn't plan on letting her live much longer.

And as she was bound by the wrists to a chair, she wasn't sure yet what she could do about it.

Then she looked to her left, and saw the Red Rose, likewise tied to a chair, her head slumped forward with her chin on her chest as she remained unconscious. The Domino Lady didn't know just what was going on, but she intended to find out. She also wasn't one to let a mystery go unsolved.

She turned her gaze to Nick Pagonis and asked in a voice untinged by fear, "Who are you?"

He smiled as he placed the camera on the desk, removed a gold case from his breast pocket, and took out a cigarette. Placing it to his lips, he produced a lighter from his pocket and lit it. He took a deep drag, held it for a moment, and then exhaled. "You haven't figured it out yet, sweetheart?"

The blonde's eyes narrowed as she softly hissed a single word: "Magnus."

"Not at all what you expected, right?" Pagonis responded. "Well, there's a tale there."

"So, tell me," she replied. She knew his type. He was so smug, and so certain of triumph, and he was chomping at the bit to brag about it. So she encouraged him, knowing the longer she kept him talking, the more time she gained to try and figure out some way out of this.

He smiled again, and accepted the invitation. "I came to this country when I was nine years old. I was a smart kid, real smart…but we were dirt poor, so I couldn't get ahead. All I knew was, I wasn't going to spend my life hunched over sweeping floors like my old man. I managed to get a job with the paper as a photographer's assistant, and eventually got the shutterbug spot myself."

He took another puff of his cigarette and continued, "It didn't take long for me to figure out that the cops in this town are all very, very dumb…and the hoods aren't much smarter. I realized that someone with real brains could make a fortune. But I knew it would take me years to work my way up from stooge to mob boss, if I ever could. So, instead of doing it the hard way, I made it simple."

"You created Magnus," Domino Lady said, finishing his remark. "You ingratiated yourself with carefully chosen mid-level gangsters, masterminded some lucrative jobs, and built yourself an organization in a matter of a few months. Ingenious. But now, fill in the parts I don't already know."

"I'm impressed by what you already have found out," he said in an oily voice. "I am truly going to regret killing you. We'd have made a remarkable team. Anyway, I set up this office to secretly conduct the business of Magnus, while simple Nick Pagonis kept his ear close to both the police and criminal grapevines, and used the information for my own benefit."

The blonde tilted her head toward the still unmoving figure on her left. "How does she fit into this?"

"Oh, you should be very flattered, my dear," Pagonis replied with a smirk. "You are the only criminal figure I truly fear, because unlike all the rest, you are indisputably intelligent. And since I could not fathom your motivations nor your goals that made you a potential threat to me. I'd have preferred making you an ally, but since I couldn't be sure if that was possible, I simply had to eliminate you. But that, as they say, was easier said than done."

"Therefore, I concocted a plan. I created the Red Rose, patterning her on you. I knew she would pique your interest, and eventually bring you to me."

"So she's been in on this with you the entire time?" the blonde queried.

"Oh, no…that's the best part of this. She's entirely legitimate, and believes she's been battling crime…with the aid of Nick Pagonis and his invaluable contacts, of course. I'd introduce you to her, but she seems to still be in slumberland. Her name is Margaret Temple. Grew up on a ranch in Wyoming, a real rough and tumble tomboy…until she turned sixteen and blossomed into a genuine vision of loveliness. She won a few beauty contests, and like a lot of girls, had the notion that she could find fame in Hollywood. She came here at eighteen and did some film extra work and modeling, but never got any breaks, and the only interest the casting directors had was in bedding her. Her dreams soured, she was ready to pack it in and go back home."

"But before that happened, she was waiting for a bus when a purse snatcher grabbed her bag. Instead of yelling for help, she ran him down and whaled the tar out of him. That got her a write-up in the papers, which is how I met her. Speaking with her, I learned she had a very definite opinion of right and wrong, and as far as she could see, L.A. was drowning in a sea of wrong. And that's when inspiration struck. It wasn't difficult to convince her to play the role." Pagonis took one last drag from his cigarette, then snubbed it out in an ashtray on the desk.

"Let me guess," Domino Lady said. "Magnus sets up some low level goons to take the fall, then sends the Red Rose after them. She thinks she's mopping up crime, and she gets to play hero and make headlines, which makes her feel good about herself after wallowing in disappointment for so long."

Shaking his head as a wide smile crossed his face, Pagonis replied with obvious admiration, "My, my, but you are a smart one. With your brains in that body, it will be an absolute crime to do away with you. Yes, you guessed correctly. And Margaret entertained the notion that as the Red Rose's celebrity grew, she would eventually be invited to make movies, and would finally become a star. She really never stopped being that naive little girl from Wyoming."

As Magnus spoke, he was so enamored with the sound of his own voice, he paid no heed to any other noises. But the Domino Lady had heard. Several minutes ago, she heard Red Rose finally stir from her stupor, although she was careful to still appear unconscious.

And she heard the unmistakable rasp of a blade cutting through rope. For a ranch girl like Margaret Temple grew up knowing the necessity of having a pocket knife handy, and thus she kept one in the inner pocket of her cloak, within reach of her bound hands...something which Pagonis was not aware of. Domino Lady was buying the time Red Rose needed to free herself...and, hopefully, the blonde as well.

As Pagonis paced around the room, quite impressed with himself, he wasn't paying much attention to the two women, and thus hadn't notice that the still seemingly insentient brunette had finally cut free and had surreptitiously passed the knife into the hands of Domino Lady, who quickly went to work on her own ropes.

"So...what's Argead?" she asked him, trying to keep him talking and distracted.

"Why, the name of Alexander's royal dynasty, of course," came the reply.

I really should have read Plutarch, Domino Lady scolded herself. "And what happens to us?" she inquired.

"I'll be merciful," he responded almost remorsefully, the smile now gone from his face. "Bullets will be quick and thorough. Do you know why I chose to rent in this building? The basement has a furnace that one particular bootlegger allegedly used to dispose of more than a few bodies during Prohibition. You two will simply disappear from the face of the Earth, and Magnus will continue to rise."

He reached beneath his suit jacket and extracted a nickel-plated .38. "I'm sure you don't believe me," he said softly. "But I do regret the necessity of doing this."

It was at that moment that Red Rose lifted her head and looked directly at Pagonis, her teary eyes burning with rage. "You used me, Nick," she seethed. "You lied to me...and you made me a fool! And now you've used me as bait to murder the Domino Lady!"

Startled, Pagonis took a step back, a startled look across his flinching face. "Margaret...you don't understand..." he mewled in a whimpering voice. Magnus, the would-be criminal conqueror, clearly did not handle direct confrontation well.

"And then you'll murder me, too?" she snarled as she stood up from the chair and advanced on the man, even as he quailed and took another step backward. "Stay away from me, Margaret," he gulped. "I mean it!"

It was then that Red Rose gave an angry growl and she leapt at Pagonis, all of her pent-up fury unleashed. The two struggled for a few moments, and then there was the loud crack of a gunshot. They separated, and Red Rose staggered backward several faltering steps, her hands clutching her stomach. She then collapsed to the floor.

Pagonis stood transfixed at the sight, his face paled and damp with perspiration. Obviously, he had never shot anyone before. But as they say, it gets easier the second time. His features then fixed into a scowl and he said, "Well, now it's your turn, Domino...."

He never finished his sentence, for as he lifted his head to look at his next victim, he saw that she was no longer tied to her chair, but rather standing next to his desk.

And holding a gun in her hand, aimed squarely at him.

With a panicked titter he raised his own still-smoking pistol in order to fire it, but before he could, the blonde squeezed the trigger of her weapon, and the bullet struck him in the chest.

He dropped his gun to the floor and clutched at the stain of red widening across his shirt front. He then looked at the Domino Lady, fear in his eyes.

And then he fell down dead.

The blonde rushed to Margaret and knelt beside her, but she too was dead.

There would be time to mourn for her later. Domino Lady stood up, went over to the desk and rifled through the drawers, satisfied that there was more than enough evidence to uncover the entire criminal enterprise of Magnus. Nick Pagonis, it seemed, liked to keep thorough records.

She then picked up the telephone and dialed the direct line to the Homicide Division.

"This is the Red Rose," she said, affecting a weakened quiver in her voice. "I've just been shot by Magnus, but I've shot him as well."

She gave the address and hung up the receiver. Returning to the body of the brunette, Domino Lady carefully pressed the gun she had used into the dead woman's hand. She then went to the desk, placed her mask back on, and holstered the other pistol.

Soon enough she heard sirens approaching in the distance, but before she departed, she knelt once more next to Margaret Temple, removed the rose from her hair, and tucked it into the pocket of her own cloak.

Exiting the office, she made her way down the hall...not to the elevators, but rather to a back stairwell that took her down to the ground floor, where she slipped out of the building's rear door even while the police were rushing in through the front. Sticking to the shadows of the alley, she returned to the parking garage, climbed into her car, and drove home.

After the bodies had been removed and the detectives were satisfied they'd seen enough, uniformed officers were gathering all of the evidence. One turned to another and said, "What about this camera?"

"What about it?" came the reply.

"Well, it looks like there's an exposed shot in here. Think it's important?"

"I dunno. Throw it in a box and we'll put it in storage. If somebody needs it, they can come get it. But I don't know what that guy could have taken a snapshot of in here that anybody would care about."

The demise of both L.A.'s masked heroine and it's most mysterious crime boss in a blood-soaked shoot out was front page news for days. Warner

Bros. announced they were making a film 'inspired' by the Red Rose. When Margaret Temple's family came to Los Angeles to bring her body back to Wyoming for burial, it was said that an anonymous woman had paid for the casket. At the train station for the departure, thousands of curious onlookers had jammed the platform. Included among them was an unidentified blonde woman, dressed in black, with a veil over her face.

Returning home a short while afterward, Ellen Patrick went to her bedroom, slipped out of her black dress and veiled hat, and put on a sweatshirt and a pair of dungarees. The gardeners had delivered the rose bushes she had ordered, but she was insistent on planting them in the garden herself.

Her maid had been surprised by her mistress's sudden interest in the flowers, as she had not shown much curiosity in horticulture before. "Roses, Miss Patrick?" she inquired.

As she picked up a book from her bedside table, the blonde replied, "Did you know that Alexander the Great loved roses, Consuela? He would plant them in every land he conquered, which is supposedly why they are so prevalent in so many places in the Middle East and Asia today."

"And a rose can bring a touch of beauty to any place...even Los Angeles. If only briefly," Ellen said wistfully. She opened the book in her hands... *Plutarch's Lives*...to the spot that began the chapter on Alexander.

And there between the pages was a pressed rose.

The End

BEAUTIES BATTLE

*L*ike many fans, I came to the Domino Lady late...by about seventy years. She had come and gone in the pulps (indeed, the pulps had come and gone) long before I arrived in the world, and remained largely forgotten but for a few diehard fans, who slowly went about converting others to an appreciation of the masked vixen. But I doubt anyone would have foreseen what a literary cottage industry she has become in the 21st Century.

Given her popularity today, it must certainly surprise many that there were only six original Domino Lady stories published in a single calendar year, 1936. I'd been interested in trying my hand at writing a new story for quite some time, but I wanted it to be suitably different enough from what has gone before to be a worthy contribution to the mythos. I got to thinking about how if she had enjoyed a longer publication history, she inevitably would have developed a rogues gallery of her own, such as what Doc Savage and the Shadow had done. So that would be a part of my story...a worthy nemesis for our anti-heroine, a master criminal who challenges Domino Lady's greatest strength, her intellect.

I also got to thinking about the cover of her final pulp appearance, in *Mystery Adventure Magazine.* The story was called "The Domino Lady's Double", and that cover image is fascinating: at first glance we see two identical Domino Ladies, but upon closer inspection, we notice that there are subtle differences between them. I began to ponder about introducing another masked adventurer, a doppelgänger of sorts, into my story. At first I thought to make her a criminal, but then I realized that since to the world at large, Domino Lady herself is considered a thief, then it would make sense for this opposite number to in fact be a heroine.

I worked out the specific beats I wanted the story to hit, but by and large I let the muse take me as I wrote, and I allowed the tale to unfold organically. I found myself being surprised and delighted by the twists and turns that Domino Lady was throwing me, and I can only hope you'll feel the same!

GENE POPA — is a freelance writer from Chicago. He developed a love for literature as a young boy thanks to his grandma, who worked for a magazine distributor, and would bring him stacks of coverless unsold comic books, which is how he learned to read. He eventually came to devour the works of Burroughs, Gibson, Howard and Fleming, and ultimately discovered the magic of pulps.

He blogs about random things on his page, 'Nothing of Consequence, Mostly', found at shiai-nothingofconsequencemostly.blogspot.com.

A GIRL'S BEST FRIEND

by Fred Adams, Jr.

"More champagne, ladies?"

California sunshine streamed through the floor-to-ceiling windows of the Conquistador Room of L.A.'s Magnus Hotel, highlighting murals of armored Spaniards locked in mortal combat with fierce feathered savages; historically exaggerated but dramatic in their effect.

Rows of tables flanked an elevated walkway. In a far corner, a ten-piece orchestra was playing a bouncy arrangement of "Ain't Misbehavin'."

The white-jacketed waiter flashed two rows of perfect teeth. His accent hinted at French origins.

Allison Blackwell pointed at her empty glass and returned the flirtatious smile. She turned her left hand ever so slightly to reveal a ringless third finger.

"What's your name, handsome?"

The smile broadened. "Adrian, *madamoiselle*." The waiter expertly poured the champagne, the drink foaming perilously close to overflowing the crystal stemware, then subsiding. Allison lifted her glass and took a sip, her green eyes fixed on Adrian's over the rim of her glass. "Thank you." She paused for a three-count. "Adrian."

The waiter bowed subtly and turned to her companion. "And for you, *madamoiselle*?"

Ellen Patrick smiled demurely. "*Oui, sil vous plait.*"

Adrian was delighted. "*Parlez vous Francais?*"

"*Tu devrais garder les yeux sur mon verre et non sur mon décolleté.*"

Adrian blinked and his face flushed, but he recovered quickly. "*La beauté est créée pour être apprêciêe, ma chére.*" He filled her glass, bowed, and moved on to the next table.

"I thought he was right out of central casting, but his accent is authentic."

"Always showing off your degree in languages. What did you say to him, Ellen?"

"I told him he should watch what he's pouring and not my cleavage."

"And what did he say?"

"That beauty is made to be appreciated."

"You scared him away." Allison pouted. "He was cute. I would have liked to have run off with him for an afternoon."

Ellen snorted. "Did you see the ring on his pinkie? You don't buy a rock like that on a waiter's paycheck. He's a gigolo, Allison, or worse."

"Spoil sport."

"There are a dozen like him flitting around the room."

Allison held up a teaspoon and regarded her reflection in it."That's the real stuff. I bet they count the spoons after a shindig like this."

"I doubt it. Most of the women here could buy the place, you included."

The two were part of the exclusive guest list for the Margot Ledoux Summer fashion show, *Été Fantastique.*

The orchestra gave a quick fanfare and a drum roll. A spotlight cast a white circle on the red velvet curtains at the end of the runway. They parted and a tall handsome man in a tuxedo stepped out trailing the cord of a microphone. "His pomaded hair was split in a perfect part down the center of his head, and the points of his mustache looked as if they could impale one of the cocktail shrimp. "Good after..." The amplifier gave a sharp screech of feedback, which was quickly reined in.

"Good afternoon, ladies," he said in an oily voice. "I am Armand Colbert." He paused and nodded, smiling, as a brief spatter of recognition applause rippled among the tables.

"There's your gigolo, honey," Allison said with a laugh. "I hear he's the biggest womanizer in Hollywood."

"He looks the part," Ellen agreed.

"Welcome to *Été Fantastique,* the first in a series of shows we will present in the Conquistador Room this month. Madame Margot Ledoux has prepared for your consideration a display of elegant and delightful fashions from this season's Paris collection. So, without further ado, please welcome to the City of Angels the City of Light's foremost fashion maven, Madame Margot Ledoux."

The curtains parted again and a whip lean woman swept through them to applause from the ladies at the tables. Her dark hair was pulled back and wound so tightly into a bun that it made Ellen's teeth hurt to look at it. Margot Ledoux was a fusion of poise and command. Her severe hawkish features and sharp chin gave her a fierce, imperious look. She was dressed in a black, floor length satin gown that hugged her torso and hips then flared at the floor.

"Who said you can never be too rich or too thin?" Allison said.

"Wallis Simpson, I think," Ellen replied. It seems to work for Madame Ledoux. She's sixty if she's a day, and she looks as if she's forty."

Madame Margot stepped to a podium at the side of the runway and Colbert wiggled the microphone into its cradle and adjusted it for her height. The fashion virtuoso cast an appraising eye over the gathering of rich and well-placed women on either side of the runway.

"Ladies, I have much to show you, so let us begin." Her English was flawless, but exhibited a thick accent that hinted at an Alsatian upbringing.

The orchestra launched into a lush horn arrangement of "I'm Confessin,'" and the curtains parted. A svelte blond model sashayed down the runway in a sapphire blue dress with a pleated ruff that reached nearly to the tips of her shoulders,

"Maria is wearing a crinoline dress suitable for a garden party, or a semi-formal evening soiree. It features pearl buttons and a flared skirt to show off a lean waist. The matching pill box hat has a removable mesh veil to adapt to all occasions."

"Swing music seems to have been invented for fashion shows," Ellen said. "The tempo lends itself to swaying hips."

"The way they're insinuating themselves down the runway, you'd think the audience was men, not women."

A spattering of polite applause acknowledged the dress and the model. The society dames were a tough audience.

The blond retreated and was followed by an auburn-haired beauty in a red street length dress with a diagonal placket and covered buttons the size of half dollars. "Jeannine is modeling a smart daytime frock in light gabardine suitable for a day's shopping and lunch at Maxim's or a committee meeting."

And so it continued, Madame's stable of models parading up and down the runway to show off the dresses to their best advantage as she extolled their merits. Near the end, Maria reappeared this time in a saffron linen halter dress that showed a daring amount of cleavage.

"That's it," Allison said. "I'm buying that dress, no matter what it costs. I can wear it to the big charity ball."

"Which one?"

"Does it matter?" Allison raised a finger and one of Madame's staff nodded at her and made a note on her clipboard.

"That model looks to be about your size and build," Ellen said. "With a few tucks and alterations, it should look terrific on you.'"

"A virtue of tennis, my dear. I'd say you should take it up, but you're already in better shape than I am."

Ellen smiled. If only Allison knew the real reason she stayed in top physical condition: Ellen Patrick was secretly L.A.'s masked crime fighter the Domino Lady. "A good physique is the world's greatest fashion accessory."

Allison raised her glass in salute. "Amen to that, sister."

If Father hadn't been killed, Ellen thought, would I have turned out like Allison, carefree to the point of carelessness, cynical, hedonistic bordering on desperate for the next thrill? She hoped not.

Owen Patrick was an anomaly, an honest politician who took it upon himself to expose some of the most corrupt officials in Sacramento. Afraid of justice, the crooked politicians hired an assassin and Ellen's father was murdered.

She was outraged by the cursory police investigation into her father's death and the apparent cover up that ensued under orders from the higher ups in the capital. Her protests were dismissed as the ranting of a hysterical woman. When her anger cooled, Ellen decided to take it upon herself to see that in the future, such injustices were rare.

She augmented her skills in languages and her experience in sport shooting with lessons in self-defense and hand-to-hand combat, learning high speed tactics from racing drivers, and every trick of burglars and safe crackers until she could fight any criminal on a level playing field.

She had brought many criminals down, to the consternation of the police, who, in the press, decried her activity as interference and vigilantism when their real feeling was embarrassment that she solved the crimes they could not. Ellen wanted no public accolade, but it gave her a delicious satisfaction when she would leave a crook trussed like a turkey on a street corner with a calling card in his pocket, embossed white letters on black that read, "Compliments of the Domino Lady."

It won't bring back Father, she thought, but it does make me feel better.

Ellen pulled her black Ford coupe into the garage below her apartment building and into her designated parking space. Kreinbrook Apartments was an older building, but its garage was a feature that made it attractive. She could come and go at any hour generally unnoticed. Before she shut off the engine, she listened to it carefully as she always did. The V-8 hummed like a sewing machine. She tapped the gas and response was immediate.

"Why don't you get something better looking like my Buick?" Allison had once said. "That car of yours makes you look like a school marm, or maybe somebody's grandmother." More than once, Domino Lady's life and freedom had depended on the speed and handling of the plain little coupe.

She stopped in the lobby to collect her mail from the panel of locked mailboxes in the building's lobby. Nothing of consequence. Instead of taking the elevator to the sixth floor, Ellen opted to climb the stairs to burn off the calories from the fashion show's rich menu.

Her apartment was simple, functional, more like an elaborate hotel room than a permanent residence. She had begun renting the place the year after Owen's death, closing the family mansion, first for the summer, and later more of the year as she found the location convenient for her crime fighting avocation.

If she were an idle rich girl, she might have opted for a nap or a bubble bath, but instead Ellen changed into a loose fitting *gi* and launched into the strenuous ninety minute workout that kept her in top condition and her fighting skills razor edged. Once a male guest asked her why she had a gym style body bag hanging in a corner of her spare room. Her answer was simple: "Do me wrong and you'll find out."

A week later, Ellen's phone rang.

"I'm so angry," Allison fumed. "They sent me the wrong dress."

"Who did?"

"Salon Ledoux. I went in for a fitting three days ago, and her seamstress was to alter it and have it delivered when it was ready. I came home today from playing tennis, and the box was waiting for me. I opened it up, and it's the wrong damned dress. And…" She paused for emphasis. "If it was my dress…"

"Were."

"Were my dress, I'd raise hell. The bottom hem has been opened and resewn so sloppily that it looks like a monkey did it."

"Have you called them?"

"Not yet. It's the same size and looks as if it should fit with a few safety pins here and there. I'm going to dinner tonight, so I figured I might as well wear it then call the salon in the morning."

"What's it like?"

"Do you remember the lavender organdy dress with the cloverleaf bow on the back? That dress."

"Yes, I remember. I thought you didn't like that one."

"It's nice enough. Albert Wade is taking me to Roman's tonight and the theater on Friday. Why not let the world see me in two Ledoux dresses instead of just one?"

"Ever the opportunist."

"*Carpe diem*, honey."

"Those are three words I never expected to hear in the same sentence."

"Snob," Allison said with a laugh.

"Someone has to protect and preserve the language. Enjoy your evening. And whatever you do, don't spill anything on the dress."

Laughing, Allison hung up the phone and stepped into the bathroom to run a tub. She opened the taps and realized she'd left her robe in the other room. She opened the bathroom door and saw a man bent over her bed, stuffing the lavender dress into a leather valise. He looked up, startled, and they stared at each other for an instant.

"Adrian?" Allison demanded. "What the hell are you doing here?"

She reached for the phone and the Frenchman vaulted over the bed. Allison grabbed a lamp from the night stand and caught him on the side of his head with a solid backhand that sent him staggering. He stumbled and fell on his back.

Allison grabbed the phone and dialed O. "Operator, get me the police. This is an emergency."

Adrian rose to his hands and knees, shaking his head like a wet dog.

"West Bureau."

"This is Allison Blackwell, apartment eight-B in the Crest. There's a man…"

Adrian grabbed her from behind and wrenched the phone from her hand. He clubbed her forehead with the handset. Once, twice, three times, and her eyes rolled back. She sank to the floor.

Adrian finished cramming the dress into the valise and fled as the police switchboard operator's voice crackled in the earpiece. "Hello? Hello? Are you still there?"

But Allison was gone.

Adrian was lucky, relatively speaking. No one was in the eighth floor hallway when he dashed out of Allison's apartment and headed for the fire stairs. His ears rang as he hurried down the stairs. The bitch had caught him a good one with the lamp. He could taste coppery blood in his mouth and feel the sharp edge of a broken tooth with his tongue. Bad enough that the wrong dress was sent to the Blackwell woman, but in trying to correct the mistake, Adrian had involved himself in a murder.

He stopped at the ground floor landing and took a few deep breaths to calm himself. Slow, he thought. Walk out slow. Don't call any attention to yourself. He pushed the exit door open and stepped into the alley. He was more than a block away when he heard the first sirens.

Ellen almost missed the call. She was on her apartment's balcony going through her exercise regimen. She was just working up a sweat when she heard the phone. She swore under her breath and hurried through the French doors to catch the call before the phone stopped ringing.

"Hello."

"Ellen?" She recognized Roger McKane's voice. The handsome private eye was a friend who had unknowingly helped her in her role as the Domino Lady more than once.

"Hi, Roge," she said, a smile involuntarily curling the corners of her mouth. "Haven't heard from you in a while."

Silence.

"Uh, Roger, is something wrong?"

"I have some bad news, Ellen. Your friend Allison Blackwell's apartment is in the Crest on Montclair, right?"

"Yes. What's going on?"

"I heard on the squawk that the precinct was sending units to the building. I called Johnny Blocker at the station and he gave me the score. I hate to break it to you like this, Ellen. Allison Blackwell's dead."

"Dead? How?"

"Killed by an intruder. I don't have any more details."

Ellen felt as if she'd been gut punched."My God, when? I just talked to her on the phone today."

"She called the operator with a police emergency at three thirty. Units were there within ten minutes, but they were too late."

"If you find out any more details, please let me know."

"Sure, I'll get back to you. Sorry about your friend."

Ellen laid the handset in the cradle. The shock of the news left her numb. She went to the bar and poured three fingers of bourbon into a highball glass. She stepped back onto the balcony and looked out over the city. The pain again. Another life lost to crime; first her father and now her best friend.

She leaned on the railing. A tear ran down her cheek and dropped into her glass.

No! She wouldn't cry. She'd find the bastard who killed Allison and see that he paid for it. She downed the bourbon in one gulp and threw the glass down, shattering it on the terra cotta tiles.

Ellen looked across the city and said through clenched teeth, "I'll find you, you animal. I'll find you, and I'll kill you."

"*Imbécile!*" Armand snarled at Adrian, who sat on a folding chair in the dressing room of Salon Le Doux holding ice cubes wrapped in a washcloth to his face. "Did you have to kill the woman?" He spoke in French in case he was overheard.

Colbert grabbed Adrian by his hair and bent his head back. He pressed a small automatic under Adrian's chin. "I ought to kill you right now."

Adrian's eyes bulged. "She recognized me, called me by name. I panicked," he blurted, the words tumbling over each other. "And she hit me with that lamp. She was calling the police."

Armand let go of Adrian's hair. "The next shipment is in three days. If I did not need you, you would be dead already."

"I…"

"Shut your mouth! You have compromised the whole operation. We may have to close it down. All the planning, all the expense, all the risk. I can tell you this: I will take no blame for any of it." He turned Adrian's face to the side and studied it. The left cheek was swollen and the skin was turning from an angry red to purple. "What did she hit you with?"

"A lamp."

"Lucky she didn't hit a little higher; you would have been knocked unconscious."

"What do I do?" Adrian said, "Leave town? Stay out of sight?"

Colbert shook his head. "Your sudden disappearance could raise questions. The dress delivery puts us at the periphery of the police investigation. We must carry on our business as if we have no involvement." Colbert thought for a moment. "Wait here."

Armand left the room and returned a few minutes later with an older woman carrying a make-up case. Colbert smiled broadly. "Yvette, our friend *Monsieur* Adrian has been in a little conflict. He pointed to the purpling bruise. "We cannot have him looking like this. He will frighten the patrons. They will think him a *voyou, mais non?*" He pushed a fifty dollar bill into her palm. "Fix him until he no longer needs to be fixed."

Colbert tilted his head toward Yvette in a conspiratorial manner. "And not a word to anyone, eh?" He put a finger to his lips.

"*Oui, Monsieur Armand.*"

"Very good, my dear." Colbert turned to Adrian. "Come to my office when she has finished."

Ten minutes later, Adrian sat across the desk from Colbert. He eyed Adrian's face from different angles. "She did a proper job of it," he said. "You must simply be mindful of the makeup until the discoloration fades. There is nothing to be done about the swelling except wait for it to go down, but it is not so bad as it could be. Now, let us develop your alibi."

The next day, the press launched its customary celebrity cycle. The scandal rags ran bold headlines in exaggerated type: PROMINENT BLUEBLOOD BATTERED TO DEATH; CELEBRATED SOCIALITE SLAIN. The *Times* and the *Journal* ran the story with milder headlines: POLICE BAFFLED BY APARTMENT MURDER; DEBUTANTE KILLED BY INTRUDER. The respectable papers ran a formally posed portrait of Allison in a demure dress and pearls, with the story. The tabloids flanked the lurid headlines with candid photos of her in a bathing suit or a revealing dress. One caught her with a cocktail glass at her lips, calculated to make her look like a floozy.

The scandal sheets always lead with an adjective, Ellen thought: prominent, wealthy, elite, to tease their ghoulish readers. Subheadings attributed baffled, puzzled, and clueless to the police. Over the next few days, the font would shrink as would the length of the articles and size of the pictures until they disappeared completely, replaced by a new scandal *du jour.*

Ellen realized that if she were to be successful, she'd need help. Her decision to enlist Roger was no knee jerk response to Allison's murder. To find Allison's killer, she needed information and she needed it quickly. The police would be no help.

She had learned when her father was murdered that the police were slow and with a dozen people murdered in Los Angeles any given week, Allison's death would be only one of many under investigation.

Roger had friends and contacts in the P.D. and the courthouse that she didn't. He could turn over rocks she could never budge as a private citizen. Further, as the Domino Lady, she had to step carefully around the police, who would enjoy nothing more than nabbing her and throwing her into a cell as a vigilante.

Mendelssohn's Mortuary was in North Hollywood, its grandeur surpassed only by the impressive list of luminaries it had prepared for a send off for the previous forty years. A hundred feet of manicured lawn and shrubs lay between the street and the lighted facade of the enormous Victorian building, as much to keep photographers and the curious at a distance as to maintain a quiet, dignified atmosphere for its exclusive clientele. Only the most celebrated and prominent were served there.

Ellen pulled her coupe under the pillared portico, and a grey haired attendant in a severe black suit opened her door for her. "Good evening, Miss. May I park your car for you?" he said in the oily, solicitous voice any mortuary employee cultivates as part of his professional persona.

she needed information and she needed it quickly.

Ellen nodded and swung out of the driver's seat, her skirt riding up her thigh. She felt the attendant's gaze climb from her ankle to her bust, and she recognized the predatory nature of a man who took advantage of the emotionally overwrought. She ground her teeth at the thought of this grinning ghoul ogling Allison's nude body on the embalming table.

He took her elbow, and she sharply shook off his hand. Her eyes locked with his and she said through clenched teeth, "Don't. Touch. Me." Ellen stared him down until he dropped his gaze then turned on her heel. Another attendant opened the leaded glass door for her and she stepped into the high-ceilinged atrium.

The sudden quiet after the buzz and clatter of street noises outside was striking. Soft organ music, muted lighting, and tasteful decor radiated a sense of comfort that the deceased was being treated with the utmost care and dignity.

A hand painted placard directed Ellen to the Lilac Room where a clutch of well-dressed people milled around the entrance talking in respectfully muted tones. She was sure that if she got close enough, she'd hear them discussing the stock market, the price of oil, the implications of the New deal, and what FDR might do next.

Ellen passed a mirror in a gilt edged frame and caught a glimpse of her profile. Her simple black suit over a high collared white blouse reflected the proper solemnity. She adjusted the veil on her short brimmed hat, took a deep breath, and stepped into the Lilac Room.

People stood in small groups speaking in hushed voices. Urns and wreaths of flowers occupied every corner of the room, and their cloying scent was overwhelming.

Arthur Blackwell stood near the ebony coffin dressed in a black suit. He was the picture of propriety, but Ellen could see the strain on his face.

He saw her and crossed the room, holding out both hands, less in greeting her than in reaching for support. "Ellen," he said. "My God, I..." His voice broke and a tear leaked from the corner of his eye. He took a deep breath and composed himself. "I'm so glad you came. Myra was here for a little while earlier, but it was just too much for her." Arthur took Ellen by the hand and led her through the crowd of visitors.

Allison lay in a pose that suggested peaceful rest, her gloved hands folded across her stomach holding a pink rose. She wore a summery pale blue dress trimmed in white lace. Her blonde hair was combed artfully to hide the damage the killer had done to her forehead that the morticians couldn't quite hide.

They stood by the coffin for a moment, silent, as others kept a respectful distance.

"With all of the money I have, I couldn't protect her, my only child. The hell of it is, that creature – I can't think of him as human – will probably never face justice. The police are useless. I remember how they bungled your father's murder investigation."

"It may not have to be that way." Ellen said quietly. "Not if the police have a little help."

Blackwell blinked. "What do you mean?"

"Two things: first, offer a reward. In a town this size, someone knows something. Second, a private detective would focus on this case exclusively. I'd recommend that he start immediately before the trail gets cold."

Blackwell thought about this. He nodded slowly. "Yes. I'll put my staff on it after the funeral."

"You may not want to wait that long. I don't mean to push, Arthur, but I've given this a lot of thought. If you like, I can contact Roger McKane, a private eye who's helped me in the past. He's capable, and you can trust him."

Again, Blackwell thought it over. "Yes, engage him. I'll pay whatever it costs. My money couldn't be better spent."

"I'll do that."

He looked once more to the coffin and into Ellen's eyes. "This isn't the way it's supposed to be."

"You should get back to your visitors." Arthur turned away, and Ellen reached into the coffin to take Allison's hand. Even through the glove, it felt cold. "Don't worry, kid," Ellen whispered. "I'll catch him, and I'll put him in the ground."

Outside, the smarmy attendant held the door for her as she climbed behind the wheel. She locked eyes with him and said, "I was thinking that maybe I shouldn't have spoken to you the way I did and I should apologize." He smiled condescendingly, and she added, "But I decided a creep like you doesn't deserve it." Ellen slammed the door and pulled out with a chirp of her tires, leaving the attendant staring after her openmouthed.

Back at her apartment, Ellen dialed Roger McKane's number and got his answering service. She left a message, and by the time she'd changed into loungewear, Roger returned her call.

"Hello, Ellen. I got your message."

"Clear your calendar, Roger. I have a big job for you."

"So, will you take the case?" Ellen stirred her mug of coffee. She and Roger sat opposite each other in a booth in Sammy's, a diner on Sunset. The place was nearly empty at the moment, too late for the working class and too early for the nighthawk crowd. A bored waitress slouched at the far end of the counter.

"I'd be a fool not to. The money's good, but that's not the only reason. Whoever did this killed your friend. Whoever hurts you hurts me."

Ellen gave a little smile. She and Roger had danced around each other for years, flirting, but never serious, and this declaration went beyond simple friendship. "One more thing – you share what you learn with me."

"Is that okay with Blackwell?"

Ellen nodded. "He asked me to take charge. He has enough to deal with."

"Fair enough. When I know something, so will you."

"The day after the funeral, Arthur will release a public statement to the papers offering a $10,000 reward for information leading to the arrest and conviction of the killer. He agreed with me to have the tip number ring at an office in one of his companies where staff can field the calls and winnow the reasonable leads from the cranks and the bunco artists."

"You seem to have a pretty good handle on all this."

"I've been there before," Ellen said. "I watched the police muddle through the investigation of my father's death."

Roger nodded. "I guess so,"

"Can you get copies of the crime scene photos?"

"I can ask. Depends on who's running the investigation."

"I'd like to see them. I've been in Allison's apartment a hundred times. I may notice something that others wouldn't. By tomorrow, I'll have a letter for you signed by Arthur authorizing you to act as his agent and requesting full cooperation with your investigation. Arthur's name has considerable clout in this town. It should open a few doors."

Roger nodded, finished his coffee in one gulp and stood. "Time to get to work. I'll have a contract ready by tomorrow afternoon." He reached for Ellen's hand, shook it briefly then held onto it for a moment, looking into her eyes.

As he walked out, Ellen thought, this will be a real tightrope.

Allison's funeral would be in two days, Ellen thought. I'll be there, searching every face for the least hint of guilt. Roger will be there too, but in the background, blending in with the press, taking pictures, not of the small coterie of mourners at the graveside, but of anyone watching from the fringes, license plates, and anything that looks out of place. I have to find Allison's killer, and I need Roger's access to information, but I can't let him find out I'm the Domino Lady, let alone the police. I have to keep things in separate jars, and it won't be easy.

"So, Leon, can you help me out?"

Leon Clarke tipped his chair back with a groan of the spring and crossed his hands over his burgeoning paunch. "Roger, I got two more years to retirement." He closed his mouth as if that closed the subject.

They sat for a minute staring across Clarke's desk at each other. Neither blinked. Outside in the hallway, Roger heard the bustle of the West Bureau, the grinding of the gears and cogs of Hollywood law enforcement. Between them lay the letter with Arthur Blackwell's signature that Ellen had given Roger that morning.

Roger knew the dance all too well. That's why he came to Clarke instead of his partner for information. Marty Hamilton was bent, but Clarke was outright crooked.

"Numbers?"

Clarke frowned, pushing his bushy eyebrows together. An ash fell from his cigarette and he brushed it from his lapel. He shrugged and made a dismissive wave of his hand, fingers spread. Five.

Roger nodded and reached into suit coat and pulled out a pair of hundred-dollar bills. He took three more from his shirt pocket. He knew how to play the game. Never carry all your bribe money in the same pocket. If you let the subject see there was more money on the roll, the price would go up. One C-note in one pocket; two in another; three in another.

He folded the bills and palmed them, laying the cash on the desk with his hand over them.

Roger nodded. Clarke nodded. The deal was set.

Clarke rolled his chair back and opened the file drawer of his desk. He pulled out a manila folder. The tab had "Blackwell, Allison" written in block letters. Clarke laid it on the desk. "Nothing leaves the room."

Roger nodded. As if on an unheard signal, Roger pushed the money forward as Clarke took his hand off the folder. Clarke snatched up the bills and tucked them up his sleeve under his wristwatch. He levered his bulk out of the creaking chair. "I'm going to lunch. I'll be back in an hour." He pulled a ring of keys from his pocket and locked the file drawer. "No offense, shamus, but no free fishing. Work quick. I can't guarantee Marty won't be back in the meantime."

"Enjoy your lunch, Leon."

Clarke left, and Roger heard the click of the key in the lock. He opened the file. There were a dozen or more black and white glossies. Under them was a three page preliminary crime scene report.

Roger wasted no time. He pulled a tiny camera from pocket and flipped the view finder into position. The French-made Photolet used nineteen millimeter film, and while the pictures weren't studio quality, they were adequate.

He turned the goose neck desk lamp to shine on the top picture and started snapping. In less than ten minutes, Roger was finished. He closed the folder and left it on the desk. He listened at the door, and hearing no footsteps, slipped quietly into the hallway. No one noticed his exit.

Time to go to the darkroom.

Allison's funeral would be held in two days. Arthur Blackwell's connections circumvented the normal autopsy, which could have held up the works by another week. The sooner Allison was in the ground, the sooner the newspaper jackals would back off and leave the family alone and give Ellen some breathing room..

She was rereading the latest front page story in the *Times*, comparing the information with other accounts, which seemed uniform. Nothing new.

The phone rang.

"Progress report. Marty Hamilton's the lead detective on the case. I don't have much of a liaison with him, but his partner Leon Clarke owes me a few favors."

"Did you get a look at the crime scene photos?"

"Better. He left the file on his desk and went to lunch. I pulled out my camera and snapped shots of it all. I'm going to print them up now."

"Print two copies. I've been in Allison's place so many times I can see it with my eyes closed. Maybe I can see something the police didn't."

Roger hesitated. "Uh, they're pretty gruesome. I know Allison was your friend."

"I'm a big girl, Roger," Ellen said, ice in her voice. "Bring them over." Her tone precluded any argument. Ellen hung up the phone.

Roger came to her door three hours later with a thick brown envelope under his arm. Ellen always marveled at Roger's ability to look as if he'd just stepped from his barber and his tailor. When he took off his hat, she saw that his auburn hair was perfectly combed.

He was wearing a single breasted glen plaid suit in shades of muted gray over a crisp white shirt and a maroon necktie with a hand painted orchid. He held out the folder. "Here they are. I hope they help. They cost enough."

"Money doesn't matter." Ellen took the folder and led him to the kitchen. "Have a seat. Fix yourself a drink if you like."

"I'll do that." Roger retreated into the living room.

Despite her resolve, Ellen stared at the folder for a moment before she opened it. "Roger, pour me one too." She heard the clink of ice cubes and in a moment, Roger set a highball at her elbow and sat in a chair at the other end of the table.

She had a pull at her drink, took a deep breath, and opened the folder. The photos were eight-by-ten enlargements, grainy because they were pictures of pictures. The first stark black and white picture showed half of Allison's bedroom. The bathroom door was ajar. The shot showed Allison's array of cosmetics and nail polishes across the top of her low-boy dresser, doubled in the mirror behind.

Ellen's eye moved to the floor where she saw Allison's foot, half out of her satin slipper behind the corner of the bed. "Roger, would you do one more thing for me? Please bring my magnifying glass from the desk."

"Sure thing." Roger brought the glass and handed it to her.

Ellen studied the photo carefully, taking note of every detail. Allison was no housekeeper and had the habit of carelessly throwing her clothing onto the armchair in the corner beside the dresser. Her previous day's skirt and blouse lay on top and Ellen was sure that if she dug through layer after layer like an archaeologist, she could chronicle Allison's fashion choices for at least two weeks.

She realized that she was malingering, stalling to avoid the pictures she knew were coming. Ellen downed the rest of her drink and put the first picture aside.

They were in no particular order, and in spite of herself Ellen cringed at the sight of the next one. It was a head and shoulder shot showing Allison's face. Her forehead was pushed in by blows from the heavy handset of the Stromberg telephone that lay at her shoulder on the white carpet.

No blood. Ellen remembered traveling in Mexico and attending a *jai alai* game. The friend who took her explained that if a player were struck in the head by the hard wooden ball, everyone looked for blood. If the player bled, the wound was superficial, a glancing blow. If not, the damage was internal, and the player would likely die.

The head injury was all that Ellen could see. The next photo was a full body view, toes to top. Allison had no other visible injuries. She still wore her tennis whites, so at least she was spared that torment. "I bet *QT* would pay a bundle for that one," she muttered.

"Not to me they won't," Roger replied. "I work for one client at a time."

The next shot showed the top of her high boy dresser. As with her clothing, Allison had the habit of removing her jewelry and laying it down on a convenient flat surface. Bracelets, rings, necklaces, earrings, ranging from cocktail jewelry to diamonds and pearls, lay scattered on the dresser scarf.

Ellen had often chastised Allison about that habit, and she would simply shrug and say, "Hey, if a burglar comes in, it's all out there. He won't have to tear the place apart looking for it."

"It was no simple robbery," Ellen said. "Look at this picture. I can't guarantee it's all there, but I see her pearls, a diamond bracelet that I know is real, and lots of gold, all there for the taking."

Roger nodded. "I think you're right. Maybe when she called the cops, the guy panicked and ran, knowing they were coming, or it may have been a jealous lover. You said she liked to play the field. I'll need a list of her boyfriends. Can you help me with that?" Ellen nodded, and Roger went on. "And the idea just came to me. Who says the killer has to be male? Maybe she stole some woman's boyfriend."

Ellen bit her lower lip. "I don't know about that. It would take a pretty strong woman to club her that hard."

"She had plenty of tennis pals, didn't she? Could it be one of them?"

"I'll look into it."

Ellen slid the picture aside. The next photo was a shot from the bathroom doorway, across Allison's bed where a dress box lay open and empty except for tissue paper. Behind it the double closet stood open and a gown hung sideways from the top of the left hand door. The dress was the linen saffron halter dress Allison had picked out at the show.

"Something's wrong. Are you sure no one came into the room once the police arrived?"

"Not according to the preliminary crime scene report. The photos are exactly as the first officers on the scene found it. Why?"

"That dress." Ellen recounted her conversation with Allison before the murder. "That's the dress she bought, the linen one. Where's the lavender organdy?"

Roger rubbed his chin. "That's a good question. Clarke interviewed the door man himself. A courier from the Redburn service brought the dress box. They do all of the deliveries for Salon Ledoux. Allison was out, so the doorman signed for the box and held it for her in the building office until she came back."

Ellen stared at the dress. It had to be the key to the whole puzzle.

The rest of the crime scene pictures offered no immediate clues. The last of Roger's prints were the pages of the report. She'd read it later. Ellen closed her eyes and pressed her hands against her temples.

Roger laid a hand on her arm. "Ellen, are you sure you're up to this?"

She turned and gave Roger a look that would freeze gin. "The man who killed my father's still out there walking around. I owe it to Father, and to

Allison, and to myself to see that her case doesn't end up in the same filing cabinet as his. Whatever I can do, I'll do."

Roger nodded. He finished his drink and rose. "I'll be in touch."

He paused in the kitchen doorway. "There is some good news. You'll see it in the report. The crime boys lifted prints from the phone, Allison's and one other set. They're cross-referencing them with all the prints on file. If he's in there, there's a good chance they'll match him up."

Ellen heard the door close as Roger let himself out. A slow process, she thought, too slow. I have to see the place for myself.

Time to put on the mask.

As the sun set, Ellen opened her bedroom closet and brushed the blouses and dresses aside. She felt along the molding at the closet's left wall, and pressed a button. The rear panel of the closet slid silently to the right, revealing a hidden compartment. In it hung the cloaks, gowns, weapons, and masks of her crime fighting alter ego, Domino Lady.

Years before, when her father was murdered by mobsters and the case covered up by crooked cops at the behest of equally crooked politicians, Ellen vowed that she would take it upon herself to reach beyond the police and bring to justice the people who thought they were too rich, too powerful, too connected for the law to touch.

The police saw her as more than a nuisance: she was a threat, taking on cases they shied away from. Call me what I am, she thought, a vigilante; a vigilante who exposes their corruption and their cowardice. There is nothing the police would like more than to lock me up. "Catch me if you can, boys," she said to herself. "Catch me if you can."

She chose a white strapless gown that clung to her athletic form like a bandage over a flexible corset, designed more for support than for looks. Her garter belt held more than the tops of her silk stockings. On her right thigh, a palm sized .25 caliber automatic rode against her firm flesh, and on her left thigh, a switchblade knife.

Her shoes were black patent leather flats secured with thin straps across the arch; running and fighting in heels was ridiculous and for her, potentially fatal. An added feature was a steel cap under each of the shining toes.

The black cloak featured cleverly concealed pockets holding a set of lock picks, a battery powered torch, and other tools of her trade. She clasped it at her throat with a silver filigreed clip.

Last was her mask, the eponymous domino that hid her identity from criminal and cop alike, allowing her to pursue justice beyond the bounds of laws and courts. Tonight, she chose white, and as she tied the mask behind her head, she felt a surge of empowerment. She was no longer Ellen Patrick, socialite, debutante, poor little rich girl. She was a force unique in the world.

She was the Domino Lady.

Though the streets of Los Angeles were never empty, traffic was sparse in the wee hours, and no one took notice of the masked driver in the Ford coupe. If they had, she would have been assumed to be a reveler returning from some fancy dress ball, or perhaps a courtesan satisfying some rich man's fetish.

The lock on the fire door in the alley behind the Crest was simple enough to pick, but halfway through the job, headlights swung into the alley. Domino Lady wrapped her cloak around her and ducked into the shadows behind the Crest's rank of garbage cans.

The car was a police cruiser, one of the big square Oldsmobiles that were being phased out of the police motor pool in favor of a make and model sold by a friend of the chief. The cop in the passenger seat swept the spotlight cursorily up and down the alley as the sedan crept through, its tires crunching on gravel and broken glass. The car stopped.

"I don't see him," she heard the spotlight cop say to the driver. At that moment the radio crackled. "All cars in sectors six and seven proceed to Linden and 103rd, 201 in progress."

"You heard the man." the spotlight snapped off and the gumball came on.

The prowl car rumbled away, and Domino rose from her crouch. Just my luck, she thought. The cops looking for some second story artist. One more reason to be cautious. Within a minute, the fire door was open and she slipped into the Crest.

Domino stood for a full minute silent, listening. Silence in the building. She took a deep breath and started her climb to the eighth floor. When she reached the landing, Domino peered through the wire reinforced glass at the top of the fire door. The hallway was empty. No guards at Allison's. No tenants coming home from an evening of night clubbing.

Since Arthur had given her Allison's apartment key, Domino was inside in seconds, ignoring the stern no-entry warning posted on the door.

She picked her way across the atrium and into the living room. Dim light

...ducked into the shadows...

from the city below showed the outlines of chairs, the sofa and a big console radio. Domino crossed the room and gently pulled the draperies closed before lighting her torch. She shielded the beam with her hand and went into the bedroom.

The carpet squelched under her feet, still wet from the overflow of the bathtub before the police arrived.

The room looked exactly as it had in the police photos. Apparently the place was just as the crime scene crew had left it. Domino pulled down the window shade and turned on the overhead light.

Heaped in an armchair was a workman's yearly wage in clothing. Domino carefully lifted each piece in its turn, examined it, then replaced each in the chair in the same order she found it. No clues.

One drawer at a time, she methodically went through their contents. In the third drawer of the highboy, folded into a red lace camisole, she found something the police missed, Allison's palm-sized address book. Domino thumbed through it. Allison was a thoroughly modern girl. She wasn't shy about calling men. The little red book listed the names and numbers of as many male friends as women. She tucked the book into a pocket of her cloak. Roger could work with that information.

Once she finished with the drawers, Domino dropped to her knees to look under the furniture. She laid her light on the deep pile carpet, casting shadows from the smallest of objects under the bed. Had the off-white carpet been a shade lighter, she might have missed it; small, white, and when she took it between her thumb and forefinger, hard.

A broken tooth. The pointed end of a canine, probably missed by the cops because the detectives didn't want to get their suits wet on the carpet.

Domino smiled grimly, not only because she'd found a tangible clue, but at the thought that Allison had fought back and done some damage to her killer. She wrapped the tooth in a handkerchief from the nightstand and tucked it carefully into a compartment in her cloak.

One step closer, she thought.

The rest of her search yielded nothing useful. The linen dress that Allison had bought hung from the closet door. The stitching was immaculate. It was a little bit rumpled, but Domino wrote that off to its being folded in the dress box. The box itself yielded only layers of tissue paper, no receipt or delivery slip.

Domino spent another hour rifling drawers and looking at every detail of the bedroom, but to no avail. She had apparently found all that was there to be found.

She left the Crest without incident, slipping out the fire door into the empty alley. Domino wrapped her cape around her and stayed in the shadows as she made her way back to her car. She had left the car unlocked because she'd learned that precious seconds spent locating keys and keyholes could mean the difference between escape and capture, life and death. Domino climbed behind the wheel and put the key into the ignition.

An arm whipped around her neck and she felt the point of a knife at her cheek. "Okay, honey," a gruff voice said in her ear. "We're goin' for a ride."

A dozen strategies flashed through her mind. She sagged sideways as if she'd fainted, her head lolling away from the knife and her bosom pushing the horn button.

"Ah, hell," the mugger muttered and relaxed his grip on her throat to pull her backward. When he did, Domino twisted in the seat and drove her elbow into the man's fore head. He fell backward, stunned, only to be pummeled unconscious by her fists. She opened the door and dragged him from the car onto the pavement. Behind the seat where he had hidden, she found a leather valise. A quick look told her that this thug was the burglar the cops were looking for behind the Crest.

In a moment, the thief was tied hand and foot with his sack of loot resting on his chest. Domino plucked a card from her cloak and tucked it under the ropes for the police to find:

Compliments of the Domino Lady

Although hundreds of people thought they should have been there, Arthur let it be known that only immediate family and a few friends would attend the service in the Mendelssohn mortuary chapel.

"It's bizarre," he told Ellen. "Half of Los Angeles is treating it like a hot ticket premiere, and some people are actually offended that they're not invited. It's a funeral. I'm burying my daughter, goddammit."

"You're doing the right thing, Arthur," Ellen assured him, although for a different reason. Fewer attendees at graveside meant fewer trees for that one odd person to hide behind. If the killer showed up at the funeral, she'd see him and Roger would get him on film.

The small group of mourners gathered in the mortuary chapel. The muted organ music mixed with hushed conversations as the group sat in the ranks of plush chairs. Arthur had provided a list of the attendees, and Ellen was able to fix a name to every face.

Myra Blackwell, Allison's mother huddled in her sister's arms, weeping softly as Arthur stood at the coffin shaking hands and accepting condolences.

Arthur was composed and dignified, but Ellen could see that his bearing was a house of cards.

Since Allison professed no specific religious belief, Arthur asked Reverend Cyril Thomas, the minister of his Methodist church to conduct the service. The minister was a stout little man with gray hair clipped close to his scalp. His black robe and surplice did little to slim his figure. He had the same mien as the mortuary personnel, a wan smile, and eyelids drooped in sympathy.

Reverend Thomas bypassed Arthur and went directly to Myra. He sat in the empty chair beside her and took her hand in both of his. Ellen couldn't hear what words of comfort he offered, but he coaxed a little smile from Myra. He patted her hand and rose, stealing a look at his wristwatch.

Stefan Mendelssohn himself stood to the side, hands in a fig leaf clutch. He and the Reverend exchanged nods. They'd done this dance many times. At a signal from Mendelssohn the organ music raised its volume a notch, a signal for everyone to take their seats.

Reverend Thomas set his notes on the lectern and hung a pair of rimless spectacles on his nose. The music ceased.

"My friends," he intoned in a rich baritone voice, "Let us pray."

Ellen heard little of the minister's packet of platitudes. Her mind was racing, collating information, weighing clues, and churning with frustration.

At the final amen, Mendelssohn's staff closed the casket and escorted the mourners to a line of black limousines. Ellen rode with Arthur, Myra, and Allison's aunt. As they rolled through the gates of the mortuary, flashbulbs popped and the reporters peered through the windows.

Ghouls, Ellen thought. Then she saw Roger, standing back a few paces photographing the crowd, not the limos. He couldn't see her, but she gave him a thumbs-up anyway.

At the cemetery the police had cordoned off the gravesite to ensure the family's privacy. At least Arthur's clout was worth that much.

The Reverend was quick and concise, and one by one, the mourners each threw a handful of earth onto the coffin. Ellen looked beyond the bier to the press and the rubberneckers lining the wrought iron fence.

She looked at her watch. In one hour she would meet with Armand Colbert and make her pitch to Salon Ledoux. Maybe she was dead wrong about the dress, but it was the one thread she had to pull, and if it was the right one, the whole case would unravel like a badly darned sock.

Ellen squeezed Myra's hand and leaned in to kiss Arthur's cheek. "I'll call you tomorrow," she whispered.

Arthur nodded sadly. "Yes."

The Mendelssohn limo took her back to her car and she drove to her apartment to wait for Roger's call.

Roger was waiting in a booth at Sammy's halfway through a cup of coffee and a piece of apple pie when Ellen came in. She slid into the booth. "Anything new?"

He waved for the waitress and pointed to his cup then to Ellen, She scurried over and poured the coffee. "What else can I bring you, Ma'am?"

"Nothing else, thank you."

"Sure you won't change your mind?" Roger said. "The pie's the best in town."

"Protecting my girlish figure."

Roger nodded. "The employees from Salon Ledoux checked out clean except for a shoplifting charge and one arrest for solicitation. The two French nationals, Armand Colbert and Adrian Fournier who manage the shop for Ledoux International have no records; at least not here. I'd have to spend some money to check on them on their home turf."

"Do it."

"Okay – boss."

"That dress is the key to this whole business. It has to be." Ellen stirred her coffee. "But how? I just can't figure it out. Why kill Allison over a dress?"

"Don't feel bad, Ellen. I can't either, and I'm the pro. Tell me again what she said about the dress."

Besides it not being the one she bought, she said something was wrong with the hem. She said it looked as if a chimpanzee – no, a monkey stitched it."

"And the salon has two seamstresses in house."

"Two, and I can't imagine either of them doing sloppy work."

"So, somebody else resewed the seam. But why? Why would it have been open?"

"Do you suppose something was hidden inside?"

Roger thought this over, tapping the rim of his cup against his teeth. "Could be. I can imagine fashions from Paris getting past Customs, especially from as famous a house as Salon Ledoux."

"They would have to pass Customs in France first."

"Right, and maybe if the right people were paid off in Marseilles and okayed the shipment, maybe agents stateside wouldn't look so close. Or maybe the U.S.

boys were on the take too. But that would take lots of clout and lots of cash."

"Or," said Ellen, "Maybe maybe someone tampered with the dress on the cargo ship."

"And sewed some contraband, whatever it was, into the hem of the dress."

"Lots of maybes."

Roger set his cup down and looked across the table into Ellen's eyes. "I think it may be time to tell Homicide about the dress."

"No." Ellen gave Roger a fierce look. "They'll want to know how you found out and when. They'll ask you where you got the tip and you'll tell them, and then they'll file it under a ream of paper. I want to hand them proof, not speculation."

"Well, how do we go about finding that proof?"

"If it's smuggling, it's international. The L.A. police are very territorial. They wouldn't want the Feds to waltz in and take over. We have to look more closely at Madame Ledoux and her crew, and I have an idea how I can help. Tell me what you think of this . . . ."

Ellen's plan was simple: sponsor a fashion show featuring Los Angeles debutantes as the models, herself included. As sponsor of the show, she could get a look inside the Ledoux operation while Roger worked at it from the outside.

"It would take me too long to be hired as a model, but this way, I can get inside quickly, if Madame Ledoux takes the bait."

"Maybe she doesn't even know what's going on."

"Lots of maybes, Roger, but only one way to find out for sure. Let's do it."

"*Bonjour.* Salon Ledoux," the voice on the phone said in a light French accent that Ellen knew at once was fake. "This is Monique. How may I help you?"

"This is Miss Ellen Patrick calling. I would like to speak with Madame Ledoux, please."

"And what does this concern?"

"*Je souhaite parrainer un défilé de mode pour une association caritative.»*

Monique stammered. Ellen was correct about Monique's French. "Madame is out of town right now. Would you like to speak with Monsieur Colbert?"

"Yes, if I may."

"One moment, please."

A moment later, there was one click as a handset was picked up and another was set down. A rich baritone voice said, "This is Armand Colbert. How may

I help you Miss Patrick?

"As I told your secretary, I am interested in sponsoring a fashion show to benefit The Boys & Girls Aid Society of Los Angeles County."

"Indeed, a worthy cause."

"Yes, and we were hoping that we could enlist your help."

"Possibly. When would this event take place?"

"At a date convenient for you in the next three months."

"Of course, I would need Madame's approval."

"Naturally, but the show we envision is a little different. We'd like the models to be the ingenues of Los Angeles' 'high society.'"

"Miss Patrick, we use only trained professionals."

"Yes, Mister Colbert, but how many of them buy the outfits they wear? The rich girls would all buy something they wear in the show. I can almost guarantee it."

"Hmm. That is a novel approach. Perhaps we should discuss the details in person, Miss Patrick."

"Ellen; please call me Ellen."

"Yes. Ellen. Perhaps we could meet. Are you free today?"

"Yes. Did you have a time in mind?"

"How is three o'clock?"

"That would be good for me."

"Very well. You know our salon?"

"Yes. I've been there before."

"Excellent. I will look forward to meeting you in person, Ellen."

"Thank you, – Armand."

Ellen hung up the phone. She opened her closet and slid one dress after another down the hanging rod. She needed a dress that made her look suitably well-to-do and seductive enough to distract Colbert while she determined whether Salon Ledoux had any involvement with Allison's murder.

She chose a pale blue sun dress that showed off what one beau had called her "kissable" shoulders and her suntan. A pair of diamond earrings, tasteful but obviously expensive, would be the right accessory. If Armand lived up to his reputation, she should be able to string him along and test her suspicions.

Armand buzzed for his secretary. "Nicole, please look in our records for a Miss Ellen Patrick. See whether she has been a customer here before, and what she has purchased recently."

Ellen Patrick. The name was familiar though he couldn't place her. In a moment Nicole buzzed back."Ellen Patrick purchased two dresses from us three years ago, nothing more recent. She attended our show at the Magnus last week."

"*Merci*, Nicole." Colbert hung up the phone. Ingenue models? He snorted at the thought, imagining untrained people stumbling down the ramp. But the Patrick woman might have a point. The society debs had the money, and the egos. A few flattering words about how wonderful a dress looked on any of them and he could mark it sold. And it would give him a chance to meet some fresh faces for his amusement and enrichment.

A few of the right words, and Madame would agree. Who knows, he thought. Maybe it would prove worthwhile.

Salon Ledoux had not changed substantially since Ellen had been there years before. The atrium led into a spacious showroom equipped with gilded Provincial chairs and *toile du Juoy* settees surrounding a drum stage that allowed ladies to study fashions while a model posed and turned to show them to their best advantage. The drapes and carpeting were expensive and quietly tasteful, and the chandeliers sparkled.

As soon as she stepped inside, a slender young woman in a gabardine business suit came to greet her. She had a clipboard in her hand and a pair of heavy framed glasses on a chain around her neck.

"*Bonjour, madamoiselle*," she said, holding out her hand. Ellen recognized Nicole by her voice and accent.

"*Bonjour*," Ellen replied. "My name is Ellen Patrick, I am here to meet with Monsieur Colbert."

"Certainly," Nicole said. "He is expecting you. Follow me please." She led Ellen through a gilded door. Beyond the showroom, the salon was all business. They passed through a storage area stacked with bolts of cloth and a sewing room with two women laboring on treadle Singers.

One more door and Ellen found herself in a corridor with side rooms. Nicole tapped at one and Ellen heard Colbert's distinctive voice say, "*Entrez.*"

Colbert rose from his desk as Ellen came in. He was even more impressive close up than he had been on stage at the fashion show. His suit was a white on blue seersucker over a navy blue shirt and white necktie. On his finger he wore a diamond ring that made Adrian's look as if it came from a gumball machine. He smiled broadly and showed a set of perfect teeth.

Not him, Ellen thought. No broken canine. She returned the smile. "A pleasure to meet you, Armand."

"And a pleasure to meet you as well, Ellen. Please, sit down." His lids half closed, and Ellen could feel him taking her in with calculating eyes. If she hadn't been sitting between Armand's desk and the door behind her, she might have felt trapped.

"I rarely forget a face. You were at *Été Fantastique*, no?"

"I'm flattered that you remember me; you see so many beautiful women in your profession."

"Each woman is unique and lovely in her own way. It is my job to make them more so."

The door opened, and Nicole brought in a tray with coffee and two cups. "Cream or sugar, Miss Patrick?"

"One sugar, please."

Nicole dropped a cube into Ellen's cup then dropped three into Armand's coffee. She quietly retreated and closed the door behind her.

"So, Ellen, tell me about your ideas for the charity show."

Ellen launched into her carefully rehearsed presentation, extolling the virtues of the orphanage, the unique needs of the institution, and finally her suggestion that the dresses in the show be modeled by the city's cadre of wealthy young socialites. Halfway through her pitch for the ingenues, the door opened behind her.

"*Pardon*," a voice said."I did not realize –"

"Oh, please, come in. *Madamoiselle* Patrick, may I introduce my assistant, Adrian Fournier."

"How do you do?" Adrian came around her chair and when his eyes met Ellen's, his face froze in mid-smile.

"We've met," Ellen said. "At *Été Fantastique*. "Adrian was generous with the champagne."

"Uh, yes. Good to see you again." Adrian set a folder on the corner of Colbert's desk. "The manifests for the new shipment." He nodded to Ellen and quickly left the office.

"I thought he was a hotel employee."

"No, many of the serving staff are my people. It helps to control the atmosphere."

"I see. Did he say a new shipment? From Paris?"

"Yes, They just arrived today." Armand smiled. "Would you like to see them?"

Ellen nodded enthusiastically. "Oh, yes."

"They are at the Magnus. We leased the Conquistador Room and its adjacent area for the month to stage a series of shows. We can go there now, if you like, and you can see the back stage setup as well."

"That would be great."

"We can take my car." Armand smiled again. The theatrical charm the man exuded was palpable. It was easy to see why so many women swooned over him; looks, charm, money and a glamorous position.

Colbert rose and took a straw fedora from the coat tree. He offered Ellen his arm and when she laced her arm through his, her elbow bumped the hard angles of a small automatic under his coat. He led her through the rear exit to the parking lot where a gleaming red Auburn Speedster was waiting.

The Auburn was a beauty: its sleek body tapered from front to back into the signature "boat tail," and its scalloped aerodynamic fenders gave the illusion that the roadster was flying instead of standing still. Four chromed ripple exhaust pipes projected from the driver's side of the hood, hinting at the powerful engine underneath. The white leather interior shone as brightly as the wide sidewalls of the tires.

"Wow," Ellen said. "That's some car."

"She is – how do you put it – my baby," Armand replied.

"I shouldn't be surprised. Someone in your job wouldn't drive an old Pontiac sedan."

He laughed. "My entire profession is image, as much as any film star." He opened the door and Ellen climbed in. "I hope you don't mind having the top down. I find it more of an adventure that way."

Yes, Ellen thought, like a film star, appealing to a woman's sense of theater. Even in a town full of movie stars and expensive cars, heads turned as the Auburn passed by. The car seemed to say, "Envy us."

"It's elegant. Is it fast?" Ellen said, eagerly.

"A supercharged hundred forty horsepower engine. She will do a hundred easily. Perhaps I might show you sometime."

"That might be fun." Dangle the bait, she thought, but you're still a worm.

At the Magnus, Colbert pulled under the cupola, and a liveried doorman opened Ellen's door. "Welcome to the Magnus, Miss. Good afternoon, Mister Colbert. Shall I park your car in your regular space?"

"Thank you, George. That will be fine."

"Very good, sir," George said with a two-fingered salute to the braided visor of his cap.

Armand led Ellen through the posh lobby and down a hallway lined with a bank of pay phones to a door marked "STAFF ONLY." It opened into a large room where a curtained arch led onto the stage of the Conquistador Room. Pieces of scenery, statues, pillars hung with artificial ivy, props, a high-wheeler bicycle stood against the walls. One wall was covered with electrical panels, banks of long handled switches, and curtain ropes.

"Here, you see the machinery behind the curtain. Rather like *The Wizard of Oz, mais non?* All this," he made a sweeping gesture with his hand, "to create an image, to make a dress seem from another world."

The car seemed to say, "Envy us."

"Come this way." Armand unlocked another door and led her into a dressing room, walls lined with lighted make up mirrors and tables of cosmetics. At the far end were dressing screens and racks of dresses and gowns. One rack was covered with a muslin sheet. "Those would be the new arrivals." He slid one and another down the rack, selecting a rose evening dress with a plunging neckline. He held it by the hanger in his right hand and draped it over his left forearm, presentation style. "You would look lovely in this, Ellen."

She nodded and said, "It is lovely, but there are so many to see. May I?"

"Of course." Armand stepped back and Ellen slid one dress after another down the rack, oohing and aahing over each as she carefully studied it. She wanted more than anything to run her fingers along their hems, to feel for contraband, but she didn't dare. That would have to wait.

"Oh, dear, look at the time," Ellen said, tapping her watch. "I really must be going. I have a dinner engagement this evening."

"How disappointing. I had thought perhaps we could take a drive up the coast to a favorite restaurant of mine."

Ellen gave him a coquettish smile and said, "May I have a rain check?"

"Certainly. Let me cover the dresses and lock up. Then back to your car."

As Ellen drove away from Salon Ledoux, a plan was already forming in her mind. She had seen a show card in the Magnus's lobby for a masquerade ball in the Oro room that evening. What better cover could the Domino Lady want?

Her instinct told her that under that charming exterior, something was very wrong with Armand Colbert. Why would a dress salon manager need to carry a pistol? Maybe he was simply trying to seduce what he thought was a silly society girl with his style and swagger. There are rocks under the water with that one, she thought. Make no mistake.

At her apartment, she left a call back request with Roger's answering service. He might have useful information. She would have liked backup for her night's adventure, but secrecy forbade the asking.

Armand opened his desk drawer and pulled out a bottle of cognac and a tumbler. The Patrick woman was a good prospect. She was a wealthy heiress and attractive in the bargain. She could prove to be a profitable sideline.

As he was pouring his drink, the door opened and Adrian came in. His face was a mask of agitation.

"What is wrong with you?" Armand asked.

"That Patrick woman."

"What about her?"

"She was at *Été Fantastique* – with Allison Blackwell. What was she doing here?"

"Inquiring about holding a charity show."

"And you think that's a coincidence – her showing up here a week after the murder?"

"She is nothing more than a dizzy, shallow society dame, Adrian."

"I still have a bad feeling about this."

"You have nothing to worry about. Tonight we retrieve the shipment and deliver it. Then we go on business as usual. Stop worrying."

"When?"

"At ten o'clock. There is a big event at the hotel tonight. No one will notice our coming and going." He pulled a second glass from his desk drawer. "Have a drink, and stop worrying."

By sunset, Roger still had not called. No matter, Ellen thought. I can't tell him what I 'm going to do anyway. He'd want to take it all to the police, and there's not enough even for a search warrant. I have to do this on my own ticket.

It was dark when Domino drove her coupe past the receiving circle at the Magnus and down a side alley to the employee parking area. She wore a white cloak over a black gown and a white domino mask tonight, ready to blend in with the revelers at the masquerade in the hotel ballroom. She slipped into the rear entrance and followed the winding corridors to the lobby where she found a crowd of people in colorful masks and costumes of every description.

A photographer had set up a backdrop in a corner near the ballroom archway and was posing Marie Antionette beside a dashing courtier in a plumed hat. The crowd, mixed with the regular hotel guests, filled the lobby, so she was able to slip unnoticed into the telephone corridor.

Two of the phones were occupied; one by a young lady in a belly dancer costume plaintively begging someone named Frank to come to the ball, the other a stout bald man in a business suit arguing about money and contracts. Both were so engaged in their conversations that neither paid any attention to the caped figure at the end of the hallway.

The staff door was locked. Domino stood in front of it and spread her elbows so that her cloak concealed her hands as she worked on the lock. In a moment, the mechanism clicked, and the door swung open. The backstage area was dark and empty. She went to work picking the lock into the dressing room and found it as easy as the outer door.

She shined her pocket torch around the room. The rack of muslin shrouded dresses stood as it had when she and Armand had left earlier that day. She pulled away the shroud and went to work, feeling around the hems of the gowns one by one between her thumbs and fingers.

"You wait out here and stand watch while I retrieve the shipment," Colbert told Armand, who nodded and picked up a handset, pretending to talk on one of the phones. Armand put his key in the lock of the outer door and it moved too easily. It was unlocked. He put his hand on his pistol under his coat and stepped inside. He snapped on the light and saw nothing amiss. He crossed the room and put his key in the dressing room lock.

It was the next to last dress, a mauve mock suede where Ellen found something that felt like pebbles sewn into the hem. She drew her knife and slit the fabric. She worked the seam with her fingers and something the size of a pencil eraser fell into her palm. Diamonds. They were smuggling diamonds, Allison had gotten the wrong dress and they killed her when they came to get it back. Her head whipped around at the sound of a key in the lock.

Armand opened the dressing room door and snapped on the light. He saw immediately that the muslin shroud had been pulled away. He pulled his automatic, eyes darting from side to side.

Domino crouched behind a wheeled rack of gowns that reached to the floor. She held her breath as she listened to the click of heels on the tiled floor.

She recognized Colbert's alligator shoes as they crisscrossed the room. She heard him open and close closet doors and the rattle of hangers on the racks. There was silence for a moment, then the click of the hammer of Colbert's automatic.

He put his hands between two hangers on Domino's rack and swept them apart.

Domino sprung from her crouch like a lineman, slamming her forearms upward and under Colbert's chin. His teeth clipped together and he pitched backward, landing hard on his back, his head bouncing on the floor. His pistol skittered across the floor. Domino ran over him and through the door into the corridor.

Adrian was standing at the payphones, and when he saw the masked figure dart from the doorway, his mouth dropped open. Domino flashed her light into his face to blind him, and in its beam, she saw his broken tooth. She wanted more than anything to pull out her automatic and put a bullet into his head, but she knew that it would mean her capture. She had to run, but now she knew. As she passed Adrian, she threw a shoulder into him, bowling him over and ran.

Domino sprinted down the hallway and through the arch into the lobby. Heads turned as the masked woman dashed to the revolving doors of the atrium, cloak streaming behind her. As she spun through the door, she saw Colbert enter the lobby, fury on his face.

Under the hotel portico, a suave young man Domino recognized as Willard Bentley, an up and coming leading man dressed in a white dinner jacket, was taking the arm of a petite blonde in a low cut gown as the doorman closed the passenger door of Bentley's canary yellow Cord convertible.

Domino shoved between the young lovers and vaulted the door into the car's cockpit. She slid across the seat and yanked the gearshift of the still idling car into and stepped on the gas. The car lurched forward with a squeal of tires and in seconds, the Domino Lady was speeding down the long drive to the Boulevard.

"Hey, that's my car!" Willard shouted as Colbert burst through the revolving door with Adrian close behind him.

"Damn it, there she goes," Colbert shouted. "Come on."

He ran around the side of the building where his Auburn was parked. He stepped on the starter and the big engine rumbled into life. Colbert wove through the hotel's entrance circle, blowing his horn and narrowly missing cars and people who scurried out of his way. Adrian stood at the end of the Magnus's driveway. Colbert screeched to a halt and Adrian climbed in pointing. "West. She went west."

Colbert roared onto the Boulevard zig-zagging through the traffic. He cursed as a light turned red and he leaned on the horn as he shot through the intersection.

"Do you see her?" he shouted.

Adrian stood up, holding onto the windshield. "Not yet, but that yellow car will be a standout. Wait! A block ahead. A yellow car, but I don't know if it's her."

Through clenched teeth, Colbert said, "One way to find out."

Domino had to get out of the city as quickly as she could. As soon as word went out on the squawk, the cops would be looking for the Cord, which was no common model or color. She dodged her way through the traffic to a chorus of angry horns.

She had driven a Cord before. Her father had owned one. She found it relatively slow in comparison to her Ford but found that it handled remarkably well, partly because of its front wheel drive.

Maybe she could duck into a side street and ditch the car. Domino wasn't a practiced car thief, but with a little luck, she could steal something a little less conspicuous.

Her driver's side mirror exploded in a spray of glass shards. Her eye flicked to the dashboard mirror, and she saw headlights bearing down on her.

Silhouetted against the traffic, she saw a tall man standing in the front seat of a roadster. She twitched the wheel and zig-zagged as a second bullet whanged off the trunk of the Cord. The roadster zipped in front of a car in the left lane and was coming alongside her.

A van loomed ahead of her and Domino made a snap decision. She hauled the wheel hard right and scraped between the van and the curb, putting it between her and her pursuers. The brief glimpse of the chase car told her it was Colbert's Auburn with Adrian standing on the seat, one hand clutching the windshield frame and the other holding a revolver.

Domino slammed on the brakes and swung back behind the van, her head swiveling side to side, looking for any escape.

New York may be the City that Never Sleeps, but Los Angeles is the City whose Streets are Never Empty. The traffic kept Colbert from exploiting the superior power of the Auburn's hefty engine. The Cord was front heavy because of its front wheel drive, and Domino decided to use that to her advantage.

She flicked in and out of the left lane, gauging the distance between the Cord and Colbert's car. Thirty-five miles an hour, and Colbert's car was two lengths ahead of the van, Adrian still standing, looking for her car.

Domino swung into the left lane and floored the gas pedal. The Cord lunged ahead and rammed its coffin nose into the rear of the Auburn.

The shock threw Adrian off balance, and as Colbert fought the wheel, Adrian clawed at the air and pitched over the side of the car and landed under the wheels of the van

Domino rammed the Auburn again, this time at an angle to try to crush the fender against the tire. The Auburn slewed sideways, its rear end swinging into the oncoming lane. To his credit, Colbert handled it well. He wrestled the Auburn back into its lane a spare second before a city bus would have broadsided it.

Domino shot into a gap in the traffic and didn't look back. Two miles ahead was the cliff-climbing set of switchbacks the locals called Satan's Slalom where the Auburn's horsepower would be little help. If she couldn't shake Colbert, it would become a challenge of driving skill.

But first, she had to keep Colbert from ramming and disabling the Cord, or shooting her, recalling his pistol in the dressing room.

Another stoplight ahead with traffic backed up. Ten cars in either lane. Domino swung to the right, cutting off a big Chrysler sedan to a honk of the horn and shake of the fist. She roared across the lane and bumped over the curb to drive up the sidewalk, frantically blowing her horn as pedestrians scrambled out of her way.

A quick glance in the mirror told her that Colbert was boxed in the left lane. She bounced into the intersection as the light turned green and sped off ahead of the traffic. Another mile and she'd be on her way up the switchbacks.

Colbert pounded the wheel with his fist. The bitch was getting away. Where did she ever learn to drive like that?

When the light turned, Colbert jogged through the traffic, taking the paint off more than one fender and shoved his way to the front of the pack. He saw tail lights ahead. Hers had to be among them. He pulled out the knob on the dash and kicked in the Auburn's supercharger. The engine screamed and the car leapt forward. She wouldn't get away this time.

When the speed picked up, Domino's cloak billowed out behind her, tugging at her throat. No time to deal with it now, she thought. Ahead of her she saw the bright yellow diamond of a highway sign emblazoned with a black arrow twisted into a perfect S. Below it, a small square read, as if an afterthought, 15 MPH.

The road was carved into the mountainside, not in esses, but long looping horseshoes of asphalt, a black ribbon draped on the slope. The berm was narrow, and there were no guard rails, only posts and cables at the curves.

Domino glanced upward and saw two cars on the switchbacks above her, one near the top and descending, and one halfway heading up. She was almost to the second curve when she saw Colbert's headlights enter the slalom. Her lead was slim, and Colbert was no slouch at the wheel. She'd have to push the Cord for all it was worth.

As Colbert rounded the first curve, a cop car, its spinner going, joined the chase. Whether the cop's after me or him doesn't matter, she thought. I have to shake them both.

Domino and Colbert passed each other in opposing directions, she two levels above him. A bullet sang off the Cord's hood. She flicked the wheel and hugged the inside of the mountain to make the Car a harder target.

On the next straightaway, Colbert fired again, and hit the driver's door. She was fortunate Colbert was firing his little automatic at her and not Adrian's .38 that could go through the metal.

Colbert looked below at the prowl car. It was falling behind. Escaping the cops would be child's play, but first, he had to take out the masked bitch.

Just beyond the fifth curve, Domino caught up with the car ahead of her, a green Pontiac sedan. She blew her horn and swung into the left lane to pass. When she pulled alongside, it sped up. In her headlights she saw the driver and passengers – a gang of teen aged boys out joyriding in Dad's car.

They jeered at her. "Hey. Baby, wanna race?" "What's with the mask? Halloween's over, honey!" A beer bottle burst on the Cord's hood. She sped up and so did the kid. They were nearing the next curve, the road hooking left.

Instead of following the road, Domino drove straight as if she were heading through the barrier. The kid realized what was happening, and hit the brakes.

Domino wrestled the wheel and piloted the Cord through the horseshoe in a four-wheel drift, sling-shotting into the straightaway, which left the Cord aimed head on at the car descending the slope. She twitched the wheel and dodged on to the shallow berm. Heavy brush raked the yellow paint. Behind her, Colbert had maneuvered past the Pontiac and was closing on her.

Suddenly an idea, if only it would work. Let Colbert get just a little closer, she thought, gauging the distance.

Colbert pulled up behind her, and she felt his bumper nudge hers. He was going to try to push her through the cables and over the lip of the ravine on the next curve.

Domino tugged at the clasp at her throat and her cape came free, flying like an avenging angel to land squarely over Colbert's windshield.

In the precious seconds while Colbert grabbed for the cape, Domino wrenched the steering wheel to skid into the curve and stop across its apex, blocking both lanes.

Colbert pumped his brake but was a second too late. The Auburn hit the cables and ripped the posts out of the ground. Colbert screamed as the Auburn went airborne for a second or two then landed on its nose and pitched forward to land, wheels spinning, upside down on the rocks below.

The prowl car, lights and siren still going, rounded the hairpin and slid to a stop where the guard posts were gone. In the ravine, flames licked around the Auburn's frame, and the gas tank exploded into a ball of fire with a dull whump.

Above them, Domino rounded the final curve and sped away before the cops got on the squawk and called in half the force.

She had to ditch the Cord. Not only was it conspicuous because of its color, it was conspicuous because of dented fenders, shattered glass, and bullet holes. But first, she had to get off the mountain. Her change of dress, tucked into her cloak, was lost, burned, she hoped, with Colbert's car.

At the mountaintop, the road split three ways into pricey estates. She took the middle road past a sign that read Laurel Heights, knowing that a road led down the mountain on the other side.

Domino drove past mansions as big or bigger than the one her father had left her, wondering whether the people behind these walls and gates slept any better than she, knowing their wealth made them the targets of the have nots; whether by the larceny of robbery or by the larceny of big business.

The other side of the mountain was as different as the other side of the Moon. Truck farms and fields sprawled below in the moonlight. She wanted to pick a road, any road and just drive and drive and drive, to leave it all behind her and never look back, but she knew she couldn't. There was more to be done.

Domino turned onto a two-lane road that led to an L.A. suburb. How did the Robert Frost poem put it? "Miles to go before I sleep . . ."

Domino finally left the Cord in the back row of a used car lot, but not before she wiped down the car's interior and doors to leave no prints. Once out of the car, she doffed the mask and flagged down a cab two blocks from the lot.

Robert, her building's doorman, opened the door of the taxi and looked modestly away as she reached into the *décolleté* of her dress to pull out a five dollar bill for the cabbie. He touched the brim of his cap and held the door as she went into the building's foyer. "Goodnight, Miss Patrick."

Ellen mumbled a thank you and stepped into the elevator. The doors rumbled shut, and she sagged backward against the cool metal panels of the car. Miss Patrick. Ellen Patrick. Domino Lady. It was like schizophrenia; how much longer could she keep the two identities separate before one conquered the other?

You're tired, Ellen, she told herself. Very, very tired. In the thick of the action, adrenaline had fueled her fight and her flight, but now that it was over, she felt a numbing weariness creep over her.

She had come close to being killed many times as the Domino Lady, but it had never been so close a thing as it had this night. And she'd killed two men. Though it was kill or be murdered, it was still not something to be taken lightly.

At her floor, Ellen was grateful that the hallway was empty. She let herself into the apartment. There were plans to be formed, calls to be made, but they would have to wait. She lay down on the sofa and closed her eyes, and in seconds Ellen was sound asleep.

The phone woke her. The sheer curtains glowed in the morning sun.

It was Roger. "Ellen?"

"Roger, what time is it?"

"Seven-thirty. I was in Sacramento all day getting a line on Salon Ledoux as a foreign company operating on American soil. I tried to call you when I got back, but you weren't home."

"I was out."

"Do you know what's happened?"

"Tell me."

"All hell's broken loose. Armand Colbert is dead. So is his assistant Adrian Fournier. They were involved in some kind of rolling gunfight in the West End. The incident started at the Magnus, which led the cops to get a warrant to search the Salon Ledoux rooms at the hotel and guess what they found: diamonds in the hem of one of the dresses."

"So you were right. It was smuggling."

"Looks that way. From what I've heard so far, The FBI's involved. There's a warrant out for Madame Ledoux. I had a talk on the Q.T. with Leon Clarke about the dress switch. They may have a few questions for you, but I'm guessing that when they print the salon employees, they'll find a match for the prints on Allison's telephone. It looks like that wraps up the case."

"That's great news. Send me the bill and I'll have Arthur cut you a check."

"Will do. Are you okay?"

"Better than I've been in weeks." She hung up the phone, put on her robe and stepped out onto her balcony. She looked out over the city, waking up, getting on with life, and said. "I got him Allison. I got him."

And only then did Ellen Patrick allow herself to cry.

The End

THE OTHER SIDE OF DOMINO LADY

I'm always a little apprehensive when I'm writing a story with someone else's character. Apart from getting the back story and details right, I try not to hijack the character and mold him/her into someone different. Domino Lady was a challenge. We see lots of action in her stories but relatively little of her motivation, apart from vengeance on the world of crime for her father's murder. I decided to give her a crime to solve in which she had an intense personal stake.

Also, we don't see as much of Ellen as herself. A society girl like her surely has a social life, and I tied that into the story. The murder of a friend becomes an obsession with Ellen and she becomes the Domino Lady to deal with it. As tough as she is, Ellen/Domino is still a person and emotions figure into everyone's behavior. Grief gnaws at her but it is overridden by fury at her friend's murder.

I also felt that a strong woman as she is would exhibit feminist tendencies in dealing with the lecherous and the chauvinistic. Yet she is savvy enough to use her feminine charms when it serves her purpose. Domino Lady is far more than a pretty face with "kissable shoulders" to fuel the fantasies of teen aged boys. She's a tough, street smart modern woman, and it's been a privilege to portray her in a story.

FRED ADAMS, JR. is a retired Penn State University English Professor who spends his days writing pulp fiction and his nights working as a singer-songwriter. His Sam Dunne novel *Dead Man's Melody* was nominated as Pulp Novel of the Year in 2017's Pulp Factory Awards, and his Smith Brothers novel *The Eye of Quang-Chi* was nominated for the same award in 2018. His titles include *Hitwolf* 1 and 2, *Six Gun Terrors* vols. 1, 2, and 3, and *C.O. Jones: Mobsters and Monsters, Skinners,* and *The Damned and the Doomed.* His original Sherlock Holmes anthology *The Affair of the Chronic Argonaut* was recently published by Pro Se Press. Forthcoming titles from Airship 27 include *C.O. Jones: Home Front, Six Gun Terrors 4: The Town Killers,* a Sam Dunne Mystery, *Blood is the New Black,* and *Holster Full of Death,* a Dead

Sheriff novel. He lives in Mount Pleasant, Pennsylvania in "perpetual terror of boredom."

Visit Fred's website at http://drphreddee.com/author

DOMINO Lady

Pulpdom's Sexiest Avenger!

The Domino Lady first appeared in the pulps in 1936. After graduating from the Berkeley College in California, Ellen Patrick goes off to Europe on a joy filled jaunt. Her trip is cut short when her widowed father, D.A. Owen Patrick, is murdered by gangsters. Upon her return home she learns the corrupt authorities have no intention of finding her father's killers. She puts on a domino mask and a backless white dress setting out to avenge him. Though arming herself with a small .22 automatic and a syringe full of knockout serum, the Domino Lady's most effective weapon was her sensual beauty, which often distracted her opponents until she could turn the tables on them.

New pulp writers now offer up four all-new collections featuring the adventures of Los Angeles' most notorious, and sexiest, crime-fighter of them all, the Domino Lady!

PULP FICTION FOR A NEW GENERATION!

Airship27Hangar.com

Airship 27 Productions is thrilled to announce the debut of pulpdom's newest hero, aviator Radio Rita. Envisioned originally as a pin-up representation of the publishing house by Managing Editor, Ron Fortier, the character took on a life of her own when several New Pulp writers suggested writing stories of the tall, action-loving redhead. Enticed by the idea, Fortier challenged writers to imagine their versions of the character from a set of four basic physical attributes. The result is four unique women, all of them Radio Rita. Buckle up for adventure, pulp fans. She's still one of a kind.

Volume one features tales by Teel James Glenn, Samantha Lienhard, Gene Moyers, and Mel Odom with illustrations by Rob Davis and a cover by Ted Hammond.

PULP FICTION FOR A NEW GENERATION!

AN AIRSHIP 27 PRODUCTION

Airship27Hangar.com

New PULP

Radio Rita

Mel Odom • Gene Moyers
Teel James Glenn • Samantha Lienhard

Made in the USA
Monee, IL
26 February 2024

54111473R00095